John B. Adger

Christian Missions and African Colonization

SALZWASSER VERLAG

John B. Adger

Christian Missions and African Colonization

Reprint of the original, first published in 1857.

1st Edition 2023　|　ISBN: 978-3-37517-272-5

Salzwasser Verlag is an imprint of Outlook Verlagsgesellschaft mbH.

Verlag (Publisher): Outlook Verlag GmbH, Zeilweg 44, 60439 Frankfurt, Deutschland
Vertretungsberechtigt (Authorized to represent): E. Roepke, Zeilweg 44, 60439 Frankfurt, Deutschland
Druck (Print): Books on Demand GmbH, In de Tarpen 42, 22848 Norderstedt, Deutschland

CHRISTIAN MISSIONS

AND

AFRICAN COLONIZATION,

BY

JOHN B. ADGER.

COLUMBIA, S. C.:
STEAM POWER PRESS OF E. H. BRITTON.
1857.

CHRISTIAN MISSIONS AND AFRICAN COLONIZATION.

Western Africa: its History, Condition, and Prospects. By the
Rev. J. Leighton Wilson, eighteen years a Missionary in Africa,
and now one of the Secretaries of the Presbyterian Board of
Foreign Missions. *With numerous Engravings.* New York:
Harper & Brothers, Franklin Square. 1856.

If the Chinese had sent out missionaries of their faith into all
parts of the Christian world, into Russia, Germany, Great Britain,
France, Spain, Portugal, Italy, Greece, Austria, and also the
United States, together with every other part of both North and
South America ; if all the chief points were occupied by small
but active detachments of this pagan irruption, so that they had
as it were *invested* Christendom ; if they had mastered all its
various languages, and were preaching the doctrines of Confucius,
both publicly and also from house to house; if they had also
translated their sacred books into all these languages, and were
printing, and publishing, and circulating them everywhere in
Europe and America; if they had established schools in all the
chief cities and towns, and were actually getting under their influence the whole education of Christendom ; if, everywhere, they
were gaining disciples, even a few disciples, but usually the youth-
ful, the intelligent, the energetic, and were associating these
individuals into bands, all affiliated together ; if all this had been
accomplished by them in but a single half century, and if it had
been accomplished without any political power backing them up ;
if it had been accomplished by moral means entirely, and in the
face of danger always, and frequently of persecution ; if, looking
abroad through Christendom, there were to be seen such a thing as
we have supposed, would he be considered a fair or wise man who
should ridicule the movement as an utter and contemptible
failure ?

In estimating the results of such a movement on the part of
the disciples of Confucius, would it not be necessary to consider
the extent and the strength of that social, political, and religious
system built up by Christianity in all these countries ; how its
ramifications penetrate the whole fabric of society amongst them ;
how it constitutes, indeed, the very life of these different peoples ;
and how, accordingly, the whole being of every one of them must
vibrate if a foreign hand be stretched out to assail any portion of
that system ?

That the first shock to the religious sensibilities of these
Christian nations had not caused the absolute and immediate
sweeping away of these assailants ; that they had been tolerated

in their assault at all ; nay, that their presence had begun to be a familiar thing, and they were fairly at work in pulling down Christianity and building up another religion; would not these circumstances, as we compared the two parties, give some respectability to the assault?

But suppose that it were the whole world, instead of Christendom alone, that the Chinese were thus investing by their moral forces, would not their enterprise then deserve to be considered as truly a sublime one? Would the grandeur of their undertaking be at all diminished by the fact, if it were a fact, that amongst these Chinese propagandists there were differences of opinion on minor points of their common faith, and that accordingly they were divided to some extent amongst themselves? insomuch that occasional sharp contentions arose amongst them, which, however, did not cause them to abandon their common leader or their common cause.

What we have been supposing true of the Chinese, is the actual picture of Protestant Christian missions. And in all paganism there is nothing like it. "This perpetual spirit of aggression characterizes Christianity in its whole history, and lives even in its most corrupt forms. We do not see anything like it in other religions." The author of the Eclipse of Faith may well construct out of this difference between Christianity and all other religions an argument for its divine character. "Till we see Mollahs from Ispahan, Brahmins from Benares, Bonzes from China, preaching their systems of religion in London, Paris, and Berlin, supported year after year by an enormous expenditure on the part of their zealous compatriots ; till the sacred books of other religions can boast of at least an hundredth part of the same efforts to translate and diffuse them which have been concentrated on the Bible ; till these books have given to an equal number of human communities a written language, the germ of all art, science, and civilization ; till it can be shown that another religion to an equal extent has propagated itself without force amongst totally different races, and in the most distant countries, and has survived equal revolutions of thought, and opinion, and manners, and laws, amongst those who have embraced it ; until then, it cannot be said that Christianity is simply like any other religion."

The great systems of religious error which divide amongst them the whole world outside of Christendom. are thus making no organized efforts of aggression. They lie slumbering like so many enormous whales, and the keen harpoon of Christian truth shall shortly wake them up to fruitless efforts to prolong their feeble life. Even Islam, once so vigorous, now seems for the most part as *sick* as does its chief political support, the Turkish empire. In the meanwhile, what of infidelity, that mere negation of

Christianity? It stands amidst this scene of life, and hope, and effort, on the one hand, and of sluggish torpor on every other hand, it stands *mocking*, as the son of the Egyptian bondwoman stood mocking on that day when the father of the faithful made a feast for his son of promise. It lifts its skeleton arm that has no blood in it, and points its bony finger in scorn of what God is doing in the world by means of Christianity. From the metropolis of England, through all the literary world, its slanderous reproaches go forth again, and its accusations against men that have gone to live and die preaching to the Gentiles, are repeated to readers, many of whom do not know or have forgotten how triumphantly they were answered once and again years ago. But what is *it* doing, or what has it ever done for humanity? Why do its advocates never go and seek to penetrate with their flickering torches the darkness of paganism? Miserable men! they know their light could never dissipate that darkness; it is for the gospel alone to accomplish this task. School after school of unbelievers rises up and boasts and babbles wherever Christianity has quickened the common intellect, but no one school lives long enough to convert a single nation; and never since the world began did any set of infidels organize themselves and go on laboriously and perseveringly to propagate their opinions among the ignorant and savage heathen. And who would venture to speculate about the probable results of such missionary efforts, supposing them undertaken and persevered in? How long would infidelity take to civilize and enlighten such a group of barbarous islands in the South Seas as Christianity has regenerated in some forty years? Nay, rather let us ask, what kind of a monster would be produced by crossing paganism with infidelity?*

The work, whose title we have placed at the head of this article, is a compilation, of course, in respect to the history of Portuguese discoveries in Western Africa, and of English, French, and Dutch exploits in that country; but it is an original work in

---

* "They have ever been boastful and loud-tongued, but have done nothing; there are no great social efforts, no organization, no practical projects, whether successful or futile, to which they can point. The old 'book-faiths' which you venture to ridicule, have been *something* at all events; and, in truth, I can find no other 'faith' than what is somehow or other attached to a 'book,' which has been anything influential. The Vedas, the Koran, the Old Testament Scriptures—those of the New—over how many millions have these all reigned! Whether their supremacy be right or wrong, their doctrine true or false, is another question; but your faith, which has been book-faith, and lip-service *par excellence*, has done nothing that I can discover. One after another of your infidel reformers passes away, and leaves no trace behind, except a quantity of crumbling 'book-faith.' You have always been just on the eve of extinguishing supernatural fables, dogmas, and superstitions, and then regenerating the world! Alas! the meanest superstition that crawls, laughs at you; and, false as it may be, is still stronger than you."—Eclipse of Faith, pp. 48, 9.

respect to the present condition of its various tribes, and to the operations of Christian missions amongst them. The fanatical excitement of the day respecting negro slavery, we suppose, must create an interest in any work of this kind ; but the one before us now has solid claims. There is something here for the naturalist, the geographer, the historian, the ethnologist, the philologist, as well as something for the Christian, who waits for the coming of his Lord's kingdom in the whole earth. The book sets before its readers, the three great divisions of Western Africa : 1. Senegambia, with its two great rivers, the Senegal and the Gambia ; 2. Northern Guinea, with its various coasts, the Sierra Leone, the Grain, the Ivory, the Gold, and the Slave Coasts, and its two military despotisms of Ashanti and Dehomi ; 3. Southern Guinea, with its Pongo, Loango, Kongo, Angola, Benguela districts. We are introduced to the three great families of Western Africa which correspond to these three geographical divisions, viz.: 1. The three Mohammedan tribes of Senegambia, the Jalofs, the Mandingoes, and the Fulahs ; 2. The Nigritian family, getting their name from the river Niger, which runs through the country from whence they are all supposed to have come ; and subdivided into six or seven separate tribes, the Kru and the Ashanti tribes being the chief; 3. The Ethiopian or Nilotic family, so called because supposed to have descended from the ancient nations of the Nile, now spread over the whole southern half of the continent, from the Mountains of the Moon to the Cape of Good Hope, and differing as much from the other two great families as they differ from each other. The habits and customs of these various tribes of people ; their social relations and conditions ; their agriculture and their trade ; their superstitions, their witchcraft, their demonolatry, and their capacity of improvement, are among the topics discussed in a simple and unpretending, yet clear and satisfactory manner. We have one chapter on the natural history of Western Africa, and another full of a highly interesting philological comparison between the Mandingo, Grebo, and Mpongwe dialects ; the two latter having been reduced to writing first by the author. We have also a chapter on Liberia, one on Sierra Leone, another on the Slave Trade, another on Christian Missions in Western Africa, and a concluding chapter on the necessity under God of the *white man's* agency in the conversion of Africa to Christianity.

We acknowledge a special interest in this book, because its author is a Southern man. John Leighton Wilson (another of the many distinguished Wilsons), is a native of Sumter district, South Carolina, where his kindred still live and flourish. His wife is a highly respectable lady, reared in Savannah, Georgia. They dwelt eighteen years on the African coast, devoting talents, and fortune, and the vigour and prime of their life to the instruction of savage devil-worshippers in the knowledge of Christ. His health at length failing, he returned, and now occupies the position of Secretary to the Foreign Missionary Board of the Presbyterian Church in the United States. This is a position which gives a still wider scope than his former one, to all the talents of Mr. Wilson. His clear, strong judgment, his comprehensive, vigorous intellect; his learning, his energy, his industry, his perseverance, and his larger experience of men and of the world—of heathen men and the heathen world—may here, even more than there, be constantly in exercise. *There* he was, indeed, the father of a nation, and was forming their social, intellectual, and religious character, after the new and perfect model furnished in the gospel. Here, he is the patron of various nations. He has an important share in directing the operation of Christianity upon the whole heathen world. In the one true aspect of all things, their eternal aspect, his position is greater than any statesman's. It calls for, and he brings to it, a statesman's qualities of mind. We repeat it, here is a Carolinian in New York, of whom we are not ashamed. He sheds glory on his country as well as his name and lineage; yet he has been only a Christian missionary! his book is only an account of a Christian mission to the degraded negroes of Africa! and he is now only directing Christian missions to various heathen or unevangelized nations!

What are the grounds upon which such an undertaking is viewed by any persons with a secret and real contempt? The *spirit* of the missionary and the missionary enterprise is one of self-abnegation—the same which gives to Washington all his glory. That father of his country is not reverenced by mankind for great talents, nor for great military achievements, but for unselfishness. The *object* of the missionary also is grand—as grand, to say the least of it, as Washington's end and object. But if neither the goodness of spirit nor the goodness of end and object which shall characterize any undertaking entitles it to honour, or shields it from contempt amongst mankind—if *success* be the true ground of honour and the touchstone of greatness, then we affirm that the success also of the missionary—of the company and order of missionaries, is, and promises to be, as full and complete as was that of Washington and his associates. Their undertaking is vaster than Washington's. They have a right to occupy more time than he required.

We think one of the main grounds of that contempt which, either secretly or openly, many indulge towards Christian missions, is, that they are considered a vain and hopeless undertaking. The enterprise, is deemed quixotic—the offspring of crazy benevolence. To effect the real conversion of savages to Christianity, is reckoned an impossibility. Some, indeed, go further, and set down such a conversion as not only impossible, but undesirable. "There are things in heathen morals and manners which might edify Christian missionaries; as, for instance, the brotherly love and social harmony which exist before missionaries appear;" and as their "amiability and instinctive kindness and joyousness." "There is a genuine religious faith at the root of the practice of cannibalism and of the suttee and other pagan observances." "The well-meaning but bigoted and conceited missionaries destroy these old graces, without introducing any virtues which can be relied on;" and "the poor creatures lose some of the best virtues they have," by means of Christianity, and get nothing good by way of compensation.* But this is an objection to Christian missions we shall not now discuss. Taking it for granted by all our readers, that the introduction of Christianity is beneficial to any people, even for this life, we propose to meet a very general objection to Christian missions which is based upon the *impossibility* of their success.

We suppose all who make this objection would unite in maintaining that what the heathen need first and foremost is civilization: that civilization must, at least, precede Christianity, and open the way for it; and that a true and real reception of Christianity presupposes civilization, and its attendant blessings of education, intelligence, and refinement.

Now, the first question which we would put to any reader who entertains such ideas, is this: Do civilization and its attendant blessings indeed predispose any person or any people to receive Christianity in its real power or in its actual experience? Is not the very genius of Christianity such, according to the Scriptures, as that we are, *a priori*, to expect its rejection by the elevated, and its reception by the depressed? The apostle Paul says, "Not many wise, mighty, or noble, are called, but God chooses the foolish, the weak, the base." The Founder of Christianity himself said of a people that were long under the best preparation to receive Christianity, that "they should be thrust out," and that others not thus prepared beforehand, should "come from the east and west, and north and south, and sit down in the kingdom of God." He told the most enlightened and best instructed portion of the Jews, while he preached Christianity himself on the earth, that harlots and publicans would receive it before them. The Chinese are a far more highly civilized people than the Hotentots or Greenlanders were, but Christianity has been more successful amongst the latter.

But laying out of sight this peculiarity of the gospel, we go a

---

* Westminster Review, for July.

step further and ask the reader to consider another question, viz. : Does civilization always or necessarily insure the moral improve ment and elevation of a people? The Chinese are probably the most civilized of all the pagan nations. Is it certain that, on the whole, their moral state is better, for example, than was that of our own Indians before the white man came? Look at the condi- tion of the Greeks and Romans of Paul's time; they are generally considered to have been a polished, refined, intellectual race. But would not many a simple savage tribe put them to shame, in respect to truth, and purity, and humanity? What, for example, was the condition of their females? What, for another example, the laws concerning their slaves?

But let civilization be for the heathen all that any man may choose to suppose. We ask a third question: What is the pros- pect of Africa, for example, obtaining this boon? Christian missions are ridiculed as quixotic, or worse; but, in their endeav- ours to propagate Christianity, its friends and believers are at least consistent. But the admirers of civilization as against or inde- pendent of Christianity, what are they doing to send what they admire and advocate to the heathen?

We shall be told in reply that civilization cannot be sent or given. We know it. Like liberty, civilization must be the fruit of a development from within. You cannot send civilization to a people; you may bring them individually to it, as our slaves have been brought to it from Africa. You may break them up into individuals, and then plant them in the midst of it; and, there being no antagonism between them and their civilized masters, but, in fact, union for mutual benefit—so that it is the interest of each that the other should prosper and increase—you may, in these circumstances, civilize the barbarian, or rather, he may, in these circumstances, be developed gradually into a civilized man, the blessed influences of Christianity also meeting him on every hand. But you cannot plant a civilized people among a barbarous people, each being *a people*, and striving in antagonism with each other, as rival peoples will inevitably strive; you cannot thus bring the two together, but, whether the contest be a bloody one or not, the savage man will feel himself doomed, and will, sooner or later, wither away. Of course, we do not mean to deny, that oftentimes a small and feeble colony of civilized men has been cut off by a superior force of savages, coming down unexpectedly upon them. The case we are supposing is of a colony, fairly established and strong enough, in itself and by reinforcements, to defend itself and maintain the ground it has began to occupy. Nor do we forget how the northern tribes, which, in countless thousands invaded the Roman empire when it had begun to decline, pre- vailed in their rude vigour over its growing weakness. The empire had reached its culmination, and might have perished without their attack. In fact, they brought to it new elements of life and vigour. Perhaps if we were acquainted perfectly with all that goes to constitute the truth upon this nice question, we might conclude that the Germans were, in some respects, as civilized as the Romans. However this may be, it is certain that the Rome they conquered did yet subdue them. Weak as were its powers of digestion, it nevertheless assimilated them to itself, and so the civilized man still conquered the savage.* Nor yet have we forgotten that other savage invasion, if we may so call it, of civilized Europe—that far more energetic and enthusiastic invasion by the Saracens, in which, as Guizot says, "the spirit of conquest and the spirit of proselytism were united"—that invasion which was "undertaken with moral passions and ideas," with the "power of the sword and the power of the word" conjoined. But that was a very peculiar case, precisely because the Arabs came "both as conquerors and as missionaries." And it is to be doubted indeed, whether, after all, they were, at that time, a much less developed race, either morally or mentally, than were the people they invaded.

What we do mean to assert, and we would assert it with all suitable moderation, is, that in respect especially to modern civilization, with all its improved appliances of art, and all its development of social, political, moral, and religious ideas, adding, as they must do, a thousand fold to its strength over any ancient forms of civilization in a struggle with barbarism—that, in respect to civilization thus circumstanced, it would seem to be a law, that its colonies must drive before it any barbarian people with whom they come into an antagonistic position.

There is, therefore, no hope for the heathen of civilization from without. And what hope is there, let us ask, for it from within? Take Africa, and how many hundreds of years has she been the same degraded thing she is now? And in all the probabilities which mere civilization can anticipate, how many hundreds of years more must she not remain the same degraded thing!

Now, Christianity may be given to a heathen people, and she may start them also in the race of civilization. Christianity has been given to every people that have got it. It is always external help—help from heaven. And here is one great difference

---

* "Singular spectacle! Just now we were in the last age of Roman civilization, and found it in decline, without strength, fertility, or splendour, incapable, as it were, of subsisting; conquered and ruined by barbarians. Now, all of a sudden, it reappears, powerful and fertile. It exercises a prodigious influence over the instituions and manners which associate themselves with it. It gradually impresses on them its character. It dominates over and transforms its conquerors."—Guizot's History of Civilization, vol. i, p. 489.

between our Christian philosophy, respecting the state and prospects of the heathen, and the philosophy of those who think civilization must go and prepare the way for Christianity. We hold that no moral development from within man, unassisted from heaven, ever really benefitted man. We hold that there are no upward tendencies in any people of themselves, and most manifestly and especially, that there are no upward tendencies in any modern heathen nation, irrespective of external influences. And we hold that God has extended a helping hand to man in the Gospel of Jesus Christ—a helping hand the most direct, the most positive, the most efficient, the most gracious, that ever was extended from heaven.

Let us go a little further in setting forth our philosophy respecting the heathen. As we hold that the help of God is the one and only hope of heathen man, so too we hold that the measure of its being extended to any people, and of its being made efficient among that people, is the sovereign will and pleasure of the Almighty. That Christianity is to prevail finally in the whole earth, we understand Him to have promised in His word; but we do not read that He designs to save all men now living, or to elevate by means of Christianity and by civilization following it, all the nations at present existing. In the person of His Son Jesus Christ He instituted, while on this earth, an order of men whose calling is to preach His word; and commanded His church to send that word to every nation. But He has not said, so far as we know, that when His servants go and preach, the heathen shall all hear and believe. It may be His sovereign pleasure to effect the national conversion, or it may seem good to Him to call individually out of heathen darkness only some portion of the nation; even as it has always been His method to build up His kingdom in this world, not *by nations* but *by individuals*, calling them as individuals, and as such joining them to that holy nation and that peculiar people over which He is King. In the South Sea Islands, for example, there has been a conversion of the nations. Those governments are Christian; their laws accord with Christianity. But even in those islands it is only *individuals* that can be regarded as true Christians. Now the point we insist on, after having stated our philosophy respecting the heathen, is, that if it be true, indeed, as has lately been alleged, that many of these professed converts to Christianity are still heathen at heart, and in their dark recesses still practice heathen rites, this is no proof of the failure of Christian missions. Why should we expect Christianity among the heathen to accomplish what her Divine Head has not promised to accomplish by her anywhere upon the earth? Are there not in every country, hypocrites doing in secret what openly they repudiate? But we are very willing at any time to enter into a comparison of the actual success of Christianity amongst the heathen with any efforts of civilization for their benefit. The statement of what the latter has done for any heathen people must indeed be a very short one, as there is no such thing as civilization coming to any people from without, as the actual contact of a civilized people with a savage people has always been to the damage of the latter. We do not recall a case in all history where the colonization of civilized men amongst barbarians ever operated to the benefit of those barbarians. Even colonies of Christian people in distinction from missions of Christian ministers have, so far as we know, never gone to any heathen shore, except as the forerunners of destruction to its inhabitants. We are of opinion that the colony of American blacks at Liberia will be found, in the end, no exception to this general law. Mr. Wilson, in the work under review, warns the Colonization Society that this will be, without great care, the effect of their labours. He makes also some other observations on the scheme of African colonization, which we consider eminently judicious. We regard that scheme as particularly open to objection from the standpoint of our present theme. As being a scheme to propagate Christianity by means of civilization; as being a scheme which puts civilization on a level with Christianity, if not in advance of Christianity, with respect to the improvement of the heathen of Africa, it is just here we find the weakest of all the weak places in that undertaking. We propose to discuss the whole question of African colonization before we close, and we drop the subject for the present.

Returning to the point in hand, viz., the comparative benefits of Christianity and civilization among the heathen, we meet an accusation against the former which has been recently urged with a virulent zeal, but which we have anticipated and disposed of in the preceding paragraph. The charge is, that whereas there were formerly in the Sandwich Islands four hundred thousand people, now that Christianity has entered only sixty-five thousand remain. It is admitted by the accusers, that after the discovery of those islands by Europeans, there was the addition of physical and moral mischiefs, diseases, and intemperance; which, acting upon the established licentiousness, might account for even such a depopulation as is recorded.* But it is urged, that the depopulation has been greater than ever since the introduction of Christianity, although she claims to have put an end to "war, and to infanticide, and to recklessness of life." This depopulation is, in the first place, traced to the fact that all their "customs were

---

* Westminster Review, for July, 1856.

changed and their pleasures taken away" by the missions. A second way in which, it is said, they have caused this depopulation, is that the naked people have been taught to put on clothes. It seems that this has "rendered them liable to consumption." Another of the depopulating influences of Christianity, is that their heathen and licentious "sports and festivals have been suppressed," which causes them to mope and die. Another way in which the advent of Christianity has been disastrous, is that the missionaries and the nobles live in so much luxury, that the rest of the people are "underfed," and have to "suffer a chronic hunger which their fathers never knew." The fifth and last charge against Christianity, is of a piece with these other four. It is, that the missionaries oppose what is known as the custom of "local husbands," and also preach against fornication, and punish sensuality with church censures; and hence whenever wicked civilized foreigners lead astray native females, the "public shame" which follows is, of course, the fault of the missionary. And so, too, the infanticide resorted to in order to escape from that shame is the fault of the missionary! And therefore because infanticide, of course, helps depopulation, that depopulation which is going on at the Sandwich Islands is to be laid at the door of Christian missions!

To state, is to refute such objections to Christian missions at the bar of all common sense and candour. The depopulation of the Sandwich Islands is indeed a melancholy spectacle. There is in it all, however, nothing different from the universal law of colonization. The missionary has not been alone at the Sandwich Islands. Civilization, too, has gone there—civilization, as represented by a large body of American and of European settlers. And civilization, which could not be given to them from without, could nevertheless blight them, as it always does, and must blight the barbarian that comes into antagonism with the civilized man. And if this be the law of colonization; if it be ordained by the Creator, that, whether with or without bloody warfare, the savage people must fade before the civilized people; while we drop a tear of pity for the "poor Indian" and the poor savage of every name, that submissively bows before his irreversible fate, and retires out of sight, we do not understand how this matter can be fairly brought into the war against Christian missions. If that be God's plan and purpose, we do not know that it is revealed by Him anywhere in the Scriptures. It is revealed by Him in the book of His providence only. But we are not of those who reject either revelation. We humbly receive whatever He reveals in either book. We bow submissively to it all, for we cannot presume to judge Him. If it be His purpose to fill the world with a superior race for the glory of the millenium to dawn upon, we do not see why that should damp our zeal for saving, as far as posssble, the present fading races. His written word commands us to go and preach the gospel to them. All we have to do is humbly to obey, and, filled with awe of His terribleness and with adoring gratitude for His grace, to feel that all our toils and sacrifices are ten thousand times repaid, if we can be the means of saving only some individuals of them ere they pass away.

If the reader would justly apprehend the success of Christian missions, let him consider fairly the present state of the case.

1. Many important points have been already occupied. From these points the light is radiating in all directions. It is getting brighter continually at all these chief points, and at other new points continually fresh lights are being kindled. Is there not, therefore, some reasonable hope of the darkness everywhere receding, at last, before the light?

2. Much preparatory work has been accomplished, which could not, except by miracle, have been done without time and labour. The apostles had miraculously given to them the knowledge of tongues, but the modern missionary must patiently learn them. And so, the Scriptures must be laboriously translated and printed. And so, the slow processes of education must be carried on, for years, in order to have a soil prepared for the good seed. And so, there must be a slow and patient acquiring of the confidence and respect of the heathen. Their prejudices must be *lived down*, by years of kindness, and of probity, and patient endurance of their reproaches. Now these are some of the preparatory works which were indispensable to a *beginning* of the missionary work. And these have all been to some extent accomplished.

3. But there was a preparatory work to be done also in the church at home. She was to be roused. She was also to be trained. A generation must be trained at home who should know how *to give*, and also a generation who should know how *to go*, that the gospel might be preached to the heathen. Something has been done in these preparatory works.

4. Meanwhile, the providence of God has been marvellously coöperating with the church. China and Turkey (and we may add India too), closed to the Christian missionary thirty years ago, are now thrown open to him. In Turkey the fullest toleration of Christianity is the established policy of government. In the meanwhile, commerce and the arts are in an hundred different ways made subservient by God's providence to the work of Christian missions. And yet these encouraging features of the case, we would not have the reader contemplate alone. Other views must be taken along with these, in order to a just conception of the case. "We have laboured, prayed, and hoped," says a missionary in India, "for their conversion, expecting God, in his own time, to

take out of them a people for His name! Some hear us attentively, attend our Sabbath preaching, read the New Testament, and sometimes ask us to pray for them. But, on the other hand, I see the evil influence of Hinduism, Mohammedanism, and Pantheism, on the character of the people in such a way, that I am led to fear the masses are generally sinking under these influences." "Our work is just begun," says another; "while a few names are added to our church yearly, myriads are added to the swarming ranks of heathenism. We could have no hope, but the Lord of Hosts." Here, as with a needle, does this missionary touch the very point of weakness in the whole enterprise, considered in a mere human point of view; which is, that in the very moment that they, *by God's blessing, convert one heathen, and he is translated out of the kingdom of darkness into that of light, hundreds are in that very moment born naturally into a state of sin and misery. So that, instead of gaining ground, Christianity is actually losing ground every moment. This is a difficulty in the way of the success of Christian missions which their adversaries seem not to have considered. It is greater than all their enumerated difficulties put together. Yet is even this nothing, before the invincible cause of Christianity; because, as said the missionary, "our hope is in the Lord of Hosts." For Him, "nothing is too hard." He can "convert a nation in a day."

But there remains a second main ground of contempt for Christian missions, upon which we would offer a few observations. This is the opinion, that the enterprise as commonly understood and pursued by its friends, is a melancholy, baseless, and fanatical delusion. Christians, generally, believe that all heathen men and women, dying such, are lost. The great motive power of the whole undertaking is this belief. It must be confessed that, with a lamentable inconsistency on the part of the Christian church, this awful belief, like some other Christian beliefs, operates very feebly. Yet, what else, we would ask, is operating at all for the good of any heathen people? Let civilization or philosophy point to any benevolent or unselfish efforts whatsoever, on the part of either of them, to improve savage men.

But this old and well nigh universal belief of the Christian church is represented in some quarters as belonging only to the dark ages. For this enlightened age, such an idea does not answer. We are too civilized, we are too liberal, and too humane for it. In vain do old-fashioned Christians point to the express language of the Bible. In vain do they produce positive testimony from the Apostle Paul, or argue from various declarations of our Saviour, and from His ascending command to preach to every creature. There is a tribunal of appeal in this age, higher than the Bible—and that is human reason and human sympathy.

The moral intuitions of humanity can better teach us the future of the heathen, than can God himself.

The readers of this journal dwell in all old-fashioned section ot the country. We are behind the age, undoubtedly, in many of its improvements. We have not yet given up our Bible, although we confess that we come very far short of obedience to the rules of that book. We still venerate it as a perfect standard of faith and obedience. When modern civilization condemns slavery as a barbarous and wicked institution, we go to *the Word*, and, finding it there sanctioned by the God of Abraham, and by our Lord Jesus Christ, we do not suffer a sickly sentimentalism to explain away the distinct language of that inspired volume. And when the same modern philanthropy, more humane and more merciful than God reveals Himself to be, would explain away what the same Word says, respecting the heathen, we will still hold fast to our Bibles. That Divine book is not good enough for abolitionists, nor for any other sect of the brotherhood of human reason and human charity, but it is good enough for us. We want no better Bible, and no better God.

It is worthy of notice how the denial that the heathen are in any danger of perishing, which has recently appeared in a certain quarter, is accompanied by the denial that Christianity does the heathen any good, or makes them any better. The idea is broadly held forth, that the heathen are better as they are, than Christians themselves. Christian missions "destroy what is good among them, and put only evil in its place." "At the bottom of the suttee and of cannibalism, there is a genuine religious faith;" but at the bottom of Christian missions and of the Christian faith which produces them, there is only folly and fraud. It is not very long since we were informed from the same quarter that the "early books of the Old Testament abound with misapprehensions of the meaning of ancient astronomical and chronological emblems, and with imaginative interpretations and misreadings of hieroglyphical records; that "the Pentateuch is a miscellaneous collection of fragmentary records—a compilation of old documents, interspersed with narrations founded on oral traditions;" that the story of the serpent reads "like one of the numerous myths which arose out of the zodiacal emblems;" that "the story of Joshua is one of the whimsical mistakes in the progress of the change from the pictorial hieroglyphic to the phonetic mode of writing;" and that "in fact, Christ himself denied the infallibility of the Jewish Scriptures, and was nailed to the cross, in great part, on account of this 'infidelity.'"

From the same humane, meek, and liberal quarter, also was promulgated not long since, the following imprecation of "death without mercy" upon the Christian clergy—well illustrating what Robert Hall called the real *ferocity* of infidelity :

"The crime of depriving a fellow-creature of life, is not the effce of greatest magnitude of which any human being can be guilty. If capital punishment be allowable for that, then would death without mercy—the death of the Mosaic law, death by stoning—be the appropriate penalty, not of Sabbath breaking, but of trafficking in superstition ; trading in man's weakness, and with his· loftiest aspirations ; converting his instincts of awe and reverence for the wonderful and admirable, into abject terrors ; his most sacred emotions of grief, his solemn moments of parting on the confines of eternity, his very hopes of immortality, into implements of a craft, a source of income, a miserable instrument of popularity and power ; and, the object attained, endeavouring to perpetuate it by proclaiming the infallibility of creeds and canons, persecuting those who question it as infidels to God, resisting the extension of knowledge among the masses, or rendering it exclusive and nominal, and thus seeking to crush the human mind under the wheels of the modern Juggernaut of conventional idolatry."

We are aware, of course, that doubts of the Christian doctrine respecting the future of the heathen, extend to many persons who have no sympathy with infidelity. Even amongst the supporters of Christian missions, some take the low view lately put forth, to our surprise, in a very respectable quarter in the north of Britain :

"We shudder at the accounts of devil-worshippers which come to us from so many mission-fields. We pity the dreary delusion of the Manichees, who enthroned the evil principle in heaven. But, if we proclaim that God is indeed one, who could decree this more than Moloch sacrifice of the vast majority of his own creatures and children for no fault or sin of theirs, we revive the error of the Manichee ; for the God whom we preach as the destroyer of the faultless, can be no God of justice, far less a God of love. It needs no exaggerations, such as these, to supply a sufficient motive for missionary enterprises. Our object is to introduce Christianity with all the blessings that accompany it ; its true views of God, its ennobling motives, its pure morality, the elevation of life and manners, the civilization, the knowledge, even the material progress which are sure to follow in its train. And we may leave it to God himself, to decide how the benefit of Christ will be extended to those whom it has pleased Him to permit to live and die in ignorance of His gospel ; confident that the same rule of perfect justice, tempered with boundless mercy, has one uniform application everywhere and to all."*

This theory of the object of Christian missions is not from the

---

* North British Review, for August, 1856.

Bible. We are gratified to be able to say it is understood to be an expression of individual opinion only, by the conductor of that journal. The religious press, both of England and Scotland, has animadverted upon it severely. The Free Church of Scotland is not responsible, either directly or indirectly, for the sentiments of that journal.

But it is no strange thing that some well-disposed persons should fail to follow out the teachings of the Bible upon this subject. We continually observe the same phenomenon in respect to various other subjects. As respects the principles of the slavery question, for example, it is not infidels alone that entertain opinions not warranted by the Bible. Some good Christians do the same. So, as respects charity, how many pretty things are said in these days, by a very good kind of people too, which find no warrant in the word of God. The spirit of the age, in some of its strongest aspects, is latitudinarian. The liberal minds of this age denounce bigotry and sects. In their zeal for toleration, they are intolerant of those who make any difference between the most opposite ideas. They love error as well as truth, and evil as much as good. Let them but have their ease, and all opinions are alike matters of the most charitable indifference. Thus we see how many sides there are to selfishness. But Christianity and the Christian Scriptures are distinctive; and, without some degree of that which this age calls bigotry, there would never have been and never be again any patriots or any martyrs. And if, indeed, the bloodiest battles ever fought have been about Truth, that only shows what a precious thing truth is.

We venture to assert that many of those good, easy souls, who cannot admit the idea of heathen perdition, have never considered how, in their benevolence and charity, they either make out the gospel a curse to any people, or else totally repudiate the Divine justice. If the heathen shall all be infallibly saved without a union by faith to Jesus Christ, and if those in Christian lands, who believe not in Him, are lost, then it is better to be born in heathenism, which insures eternal life to all, than under the gospel, which certainly involves the doom of some. But if, on the other hand, all those in Christian lands who repent not, and believe not in Christ, as well as those who repent and believe, shall alike be saved, what becomes of the justice and veracity of God? We wish all these " charitable" people would study their Bible better, and, better following out the teachings of the Bible, would cease to occupy, unconsciously, the ground of those who reject the Bible. There is not much to be feared from infidelity, if we can just isolate and identify it. There is a neighbourhood in the upper part of this State, where the attempt was made some years ago to get up a congregation of that strange kind of Christians, who hold

the salvation of all men alike. For a short time, the true scope
of their doctrine was concealed, and all went well. But their
creed came fully and fairly out at last, and then the common sense
of our people, and their knowledge of the Bible, revolted alike at
such a monstrous perversion of Christian truth, and they quit all
attendance upon such a ministry. The deserted building is now
pointed out to the traveller by the name it bears in all that region,
as the " No-Hell Church." It was this name which helped to kill
it. There were involved in the name, as in the creed, two contra-
dictory and mutually destructive ideas. The name made them
patent to every understanding. The idea of " No Hell" rendered
nugatory the idea of " Church," and the creed, thus exposed, soon
forsook the field.

If the reader suggest that, after all, the idea of heathen dam-
nation is too awful to be entertained, we have only to say, it is
indeed an unspeakably awful idea; but so are several other ideas
which we admit. The Bible gives us the idea of a world in ruins!
Is not that awful? It gives us the idea of that ruin of the world,
being moral and eternal! Is not that awful? It gives us the idea
of God becoming incarnate, and crucified for the redemption of His
own creatures from His own curse! Is not that awful? Now, if
we admit these ideas, can we not admit that other idea? But if
we prefer to reject the Bible, because of these awful ideas, what
shall we do with the constitution and course of nature, that is
analogous to the Bible? Are not pain, and woe, and death, and
sin, too, all of them *facts* patent before our eyes? Tremendous
facts, occurring under the government of a good God, and an
Almighty God? If the future destruction of heathen men and
women, which is plainly revealed in the Christian Scriptures, lead
us to reject those Scriptures, what shall we do when we behold
the constantly recurring fact of their present destruction as often
as they come into collision with superiour races of men? Or with
that other melancholy fact, that, as fast and faster than the existing
races and generations are being destroyed, others are being born
into their places? If we could have our own way, no doubt we
should ordain the immediate banishment of death from the world,
as well as of sin, which introduced it; and if these things might
not be, then no doubt we should prohibit any further increase of
human life under such a curse. But, if the infinite and incompre-
hensible Governor of the Universe should condescend to speak to
us, while thus presuming to criticize His ways that are past finding
out, He would, perhaps, do it merely by some such word as that
which silenced presumptuous and complaining Job: "Where
wast thou when I laid the foundations of the earth?"

Recurring again to the subject of African Colonization, it certainly is a remarkable circumstance that the condition of the free
people of colour is better in our slaveholding South than it is at the

free North. *There*, all agree that it is indeed deplorable, and perhaps hopeless. How to dispose of this unfortunate people; how to remove them from the baleful presence, and the withering superiority of white men that regard them as antagonists and rivals, while Southern masters look upon their slaves as valuable assistants, useful dependents, and faithful though humble colleagues and friends; whither to remove them, and what to do for them after they have been removed, these are questions which have long interested benevolent men. The scheme of colonizing them upon the coast of Africa has unquestionably numbered among its earnest advocates some of the best and wisest men of this country, both at the North and at the South. And certainly that is a very interesting question which this scheme will be the occasion of solving, viz: the question, whether the negro now, at this present stage of the civilization which his slavery in America has been the means of forcing him into, is prepared for self-government.

If there were no other reasons for our regarding the subject of African colonization candidly and kindly, these are enough. That this scheme is abolition in disguise (as many of our fathers at the South considered it at first) we do not believe. The abolitionists have been the uncompromising and bitter foes of this Society; and, on the other hand, many of the Southern friends of this Society have been too noble and too good to be chargeable with secret treachery to the South. So, too, the Northern colonizationists are the most sober and sound men in that region. They are perhaps the only men who have not run mad with the fanaticism which has become epidemic there. Not to take some position or other on the negro question is now simply impossible amongst our Northern brethren, and Colonization is the platform of those who do not hate their own flesh and blood, out of this mad negro-philism. From mere regard, then, for the good men, both North and South, who have favoured this scheme, we are bound to treat the question with great respect. And so we are, also, because it is to a certain extent a question, as we think cannot be denied, of sincere benevolence. And so we are, moreover, because it is a highly interesting experiment in political science. We have long regarded the scheme with curious and watchful eyes, because, whichever way it be decided, it must instruct the world upon many points that are now in debate. We have no sympathy with the new theory of a diversity of original races of men. We have no doubt whatever that the negro is of Adam's race. And if he shall succeed in the experiment of self-government at Liberia, it will be a practical demonstration of his complete and perfect humanity. But, on the other hand, we are equally satisfied that he belongs to an inferior variety of the human species; a man of like passions, of like original capacities, with ourselves, but yet wanting in the developement which nothing but ages of good training can give to any people of our darkened and degraded race. And, therefore, if the experiment of a negro republic in Africa, under the auspices of the Colonization Society, should prove, after the best and most patient efforts on the part of all concerned, to be a failure, the world must certainly be made wiser as to the nature of civil liberty and the rights of man, and as to the fitness of all men for governing themselves; questions certainly very interesting and important, and very little understood by most persons. We say, therefore, let the colonies of free blacks in Africa have a *fair chance*, although probably we should differ with the more ardent Colonizationists as to what is a *fair chance* for the said colonies. But not to discuss that point yet, let them be fairly and patiently tried, and let them have all the aid it is proper and advisable to give them. Their success will hurt nobody who does not deserve hurting. Their failure to succeed, if it is to come, will come soon enough for their worst enemy.

But, besides the reasons already mentioned for giving to this question a candid consideration, there are some others, which we very cheerfully proceed to mention. The experiment has made some progress, and claims our respect for the measure of success which it has unquestionably secured. It is to be remembered that the original obstacles were very formidable. The first was to obtain a territory on the African coast, where the native tribes were very savage, deeply interested in the slave-trade, and very jealous of all interference with this traffic. Virginia, through the President of the United States, had endeavoured to acquire such a territory, but had not succeeded. Yet a voluntary association, almost without funds, has accomplished this end. The territory owned by these colonies runs (according to Mr. Wilson) from Cape Mount to Cape Palmas, distant from each other about three hundred miles, and the six settlements of American coloured people planted on this coast, number about eight thousand. The aboriginal population of the same bounds, that is, from Cape Mount to Cape Palmas, over a belt of country of twenty-five miles, is supposed to be about two hundred thousand. To a certain limited extent, Liberia has jurisdiction over this whole region. Monrovia, the chief town, will compare not disadvantageously with most of the inland towns of our own country. The dwellings are usually framed buildings of one story or one story and a half high, raised on a stone or brick foundation of six or eight feet. Most of them are painted or whitewashed. There are a few brick dwelling houses of two stories, neat and well furnished. There are three brick or stone churches, and six or seven large, substantial stone ware-houses. The Liberian merchants own a number of small vessels, built by themselves, and varying in size from ten or fifteen to forty or fifty tons. The sailors are Liberians. There are four or five merchants worth from fifteen to twenty thousand dollars, a larger number worth ten thousand dollars, and perhaps twelve or fifteen worth five thousand dollars. Mr. Wilson tells us " trade is

the chief employment of the Liberians, and that the want of a disposition to cultivate the soil is perhaps the most discouraging
feature in the prospects of Liberia." They raise sweet potatoes,
cassava, plaintains, ground-nuts and arrow-root, sugar cane and
coffee, but all to a limited extent. Cotton has been attempted, but
failed, though it might, in Mr. Wilson's judgment, succeed very
well in that climate. Of all these things the consequence is, he
says, that "the community are still dependent upon this country
and the aborigines for the principal part of their provisions." Yet
the settlers show considerable intelligence, manliness, independence, and honourable bearing, and have a feeling of national pride.
So that Mr. Wilson, after the most mature consideration, "sees no
reason why, in the course of time, Liberia may not take a respectable stand among the civilized nations of the earth, and is free to
confess that he now entertains more hopeful views on this subject
than he did at an earlier period of his acquaintance with the
country."

We have now presented a fair and candid statement of the
claims which this question has upon our respectful consideration.
But our opinions on the subject, formed after mature reflection,
are adverse to the scheme. We desire earnestly that it should
have a fair trial, but are without any faith in its success, and we
now propose to consider the three main arguments in favour of the
scheme, which its friends are urging. We think the grounds on
which it is recommended are unreal and imaginary. We are
ourselves constitutionally of a hopeful temperament, and have been
accustomed all through life to struggle against difficulties. But
there are some things which cannot be done; some things which
man cannot accomplish, because the means are wanting, or the
instruments unsuitable, or the time for its being done not yet come.
We are satisfied this is one of those things. If asked what, then,
shall be done with the half million of free blacks? our answer is
ready. Let those of them who think they would better themselves
and their families by going to Liberia, and of whom you believe
that they would benefit that colony, be encouraged and aided to go
there. As for the others, do the best you can for them and with
them, in this country. Society must have dregs. With all the
blessings we enjoy, both North and South, we might be content to
tolerate some evils. At the South (in this State, certainly,) we do
not find them, in the numbers in which they now exist, an intolerable or even an unmixed evil. If elsewhere, if at the North,
especially, they are such, still let the North tolerate them, teach
them, govern them, restrain them, help them to improve, not
sacrifice them and the colonies, and that, too, in the very name of
philanthropy.

The first ground on which the Colonization Society urges its
claims to favor is the advantages it will confer upon the free blacks,
and upon this country, by removing them to Africa. But the

inherent and fatal difficulty of the scheme in this aspect of it is, that it is thus proposing to bring about two mutually incompatible results. It proposes to rid the United States of a corrupt and worthless population, and at the same time, by this very process, and out of these very materials, to construct a virtuous, intelligent, and prosperous community in Africa.

The class of people out of whom it is hoped a vigorous and healthy and pure Republic is to rise in Africa, are characterized by Mr. Clay, in his speech at the annual meeting of the Society in Washington, January 21st, 1851, as "poor creatures," "a debased and degraded set," "more addicted to crime and vice and dissolute manners, than any other portion of the people of the United States." (Annual Report, page 38.) This annual report quotes, also, from a Cincinnati paper, a representation of the free blacks of Pennsylvania, Virginia, Kentucky, and Ohio, as being "a pestiferous class of ignorant blacks, whose increase in Ohio would be the increase of crime, misery, and want, to a fearful extent." Page 14. Indeed, these opinions, in all their fulness and strength, are characteristic of Colonizationists at the North, in distinction from abolitionists. Now, to maintain that we can construct a prosperous Republic out of such materials, is to falsify the whole history of freedom.

We here quote a page from one of Mr. Calhoun's speeches, than which there never were spoken truer words on the much misunderstood subject of human liberty:

"Such being the case, it follows that any, the worst form of government, is better than anarchy; and that individual liberty, or freedom, must be subordinate to whatever power may be necessary to protect society against anarchy within or destruction without; for the safety and well-being of society are as paramount to individual liberty as the safety and well-being of the race is to that of individuals; and in the same proportion the power necessary for the safety of society is paramount to individual liberty. On the contrary, government has no right to controul individual liberty beyond what is necessary to the safety and well-being of society. Such is the boundary which separates the power of government and the liberty of the citizen or subject, in the political state, which, as I have shown, is the natural state of man; the only one in which his race can exist, and the one in which he is born, lives, and dies."

"It follows from all this, that the quantum of power on the part of the government, and of liberty on that of individuals, instead of being equal in all cases, must necessarily be very unequal among different people, according to their different conditions. For just in proportion as a people are ignorant, stupid, debased, corrupt, exposed to violence within, and danger from without, the power necessary for government to possess in order to preserve society against anarchy and destruction, becomes greater and greater, and individual liberty less and less, until the lowest condition is reached, when absolute and despotic power becomes necessary on the part of the government, and individual liberty extinct. So, on the contrary, just as a people rise in the scale of intelligence, virtue and patriotism, and the more perfectly they become acquainted with the nature of government, the ends for which it was ordered, and how it ought to be administered, and the less the tendency to violence and disorder within, and danger from abroad, the power necessary for government becomes less and less, and individual liberty greater and greater. Instead, then, of all men having the same right to liberty and equality, as is claimed by those who hold that they are all born free and equal, liberty is the noble and highest reward bestowed on mental and moral developement, combined with favourable circumstances. Instead, then, of liberty and equality being born with man ; instead of all men and all classes and descriptions being equally entitled to them, they are high prizes to be won, and are, in their most perfect state, not only the highest reward that can be bestowed on our race, but the most difficult to be won, and when won, the most difficult to be preserved.

" They have been made vastly more so by the dangerous errors I have attempted to expose, that all men are born free and equal, as if those high qualities belonged to man without effort to acquire them, and to all equally alike, regardless of their intellectual and moral condition. The attempt to carry into practice this, the most dangerous of all political errors, and to bestow on all, without regard to their fitness, either to acquire or maintain liberty, that unbounded, individual liberty supposed to belong to man in the hypothetical and misnamed *state of nature*, has done more to retard the cause of liberty and civilization, and is doing more at present, than all other causes combined. While it is powerful to pull down governments, it is still more powerful to prevent their construction on proper principles. It is the leading cause among those which have placed Europe in its present anarchical condition, and which mainly stands in the way of reconstructing good governments in the place of those which have been overthrown, threatening thereby the quarter of the globe most advanced in progress and civilization with hopeless anarchy, to be followed by military despotism."

Now, in view of these plain and uncontrovertible statements of fundamental principles on this great subject, can any reasonable man maintain that the free negroes of this country are fit for the degree of individual liberty which is involved in the idea of a Republic ? It is very well known that the Colonization Society will send to Africa all the slaves that any Southern master will set free, particularly if he also contribute the means of transporting and supporting them in Africa for a time ; and also that they are equally ready to send any poor, miserable, suffering, free negro from any of the Northern cities, who may be willing to try the experiment of bettering his sad condition by removing to the land of his forefathers. And is either the one or the other of these two classes prepared and qualified for republican liberty, which is "the noble and highest reward of mental and moral developement ?" The English people transport their debased and corrupt population who addict themselves to vice and crime. But they transport them to a country ruled by military power. And they judge that they do well if they can even then succeed in governing them. We are, however, to dignify with freedom, in its widest acceptation, " a debased and degraded set of people," " a pestiferous class, whose increase is the increase of crime and misery and want;" and they are to know the value of this liberty, how to use it, how to preserve it, how to transmit it to posterity !! Surely, those who hope that this result can and will follow, must be prepared to maintain not only that France is fit for that freedom she has so long desired in vain, but that all the nations of Europe are prepared for it. Surely, the South American Republics ought, in their view, to be examples of high and peaceful prosperity. If the miserable free negroes, being as they describe them, are at the same time fit to be citizens of a Republic, surely all the Hindoo and other heathen tribes on the face of the globe must be equally prepared for such a rank. We, on the contrary, believe that the nations of the earth, even those who have long been civilized and enlightened, are generally unprepared for freedom such as we have inherited. We believe that thousands and thousands who come amongst us from Europe are unprepared for it. We believe that very many of our own native Americans do not know how to prize or take care of it, and so are unfit for it. We believe the experiment of self-government in this most favoured land is at best a doubtful experiment. In the language of one of the wisest and noblest advocates of the Colonization Society :

" National independence, viewed from the summit on which we stand, may strike the beholder as a thing easily won and kept. The nations have found it much otherwise. Far the larger part of the history of mankind is a record of the subjugation of races and states, successively, by each other. So, too, from the lofty eminence on which we are placed, personal freedom may appear to us the simplest and the surest result of every proper, social organization. The human race has not found it so. It has desired to be free; it has deserved to be free; it has struggled to be free; nay, to be free has been the object of its most fixed desire, of its highest desert, of its fiercest struggles; but yet it has not been free. To preserve a perfect equality of rights, and to preserve those rights perfectly, which are the two conditions of civil liberty; and, at the same time, to recognize and maintain that inequality of condition which is the inevitable result of the progress which liberty itself begets, this is the grand problem which the nations, after so many ages, have not yet solved, and, therefore, are not yet free. To preserve our national independence; to secure our personal liberty; to advance in the career of civilization; this is what we are doing. But we should bear in mind how many have tried, and how few have succeeded in the same career; how long, how peculiar, and how fortunate was our previous training, both personal and national, for these great attempts; and how serious are the dangers which still threaten us."*

---

* Rev. Robert J. Breckenridge, of Kentucky.

But, furthermore, we are well satisfied that there is not and cannot be any liberty worth the name, except what is of slow growth. Not only must a people be prepared for freedom by a long course of suffering and discipline, so as to learn that self-controul which is essential to any real liberty, but the foundation of free institutions have to be laid deep in the remote history of a people, or they cannot sustain the weight of a solid superstructure. They must inherit liberty from sires who struggled for it, and won it by many struggles; won it not at once, but piecemeal. English liberty, which is a large part of our American liberty, gets its value and strength from this more than from any other circumstance, that it is the result of a gradual accretion. The people and their Parliament constantly gained from the Kings when struggling against their encroachments, and what they thus slowly gained, there was time enough for them to learn how to use, and not abuse. And when the sons of those sires have had to contend with their own government, they have followed the example set them by that Parliament, to which, for contending as it did with an encroaching monarch, (and therefore a tyrant,) are due the thanks of their American no less than of their English posterity; that Parliament which said to King Charles I., in their *petition of right*, (drawn by Selden and other profoundly learned men,) "your subjects have *inherited* this freedom." The great bulwark of their rights they find to be this; and they go back to history to show that what they claim is theirs, because it belonged to their fathers. And the further back they can trace their rights, the stronger and the bolder they are in contending for them. These have always been the principles of English revolutions. The patriotic actors in those great events have always professed to contend for nothing but a lawful inheritance; for rights which had long before been connected with the circumstances and relations in which they were providentially placed. And so, too, these were the principles of the Revolution of 1776. The popular idea that that Revolution freed us from British slavery, is to be indignantly repudiated. We were no slaves. Our fathers contended for their lawful franchises, not on abstract principles as the *rights of men*, but on legal principles as the *rights of Englishmen,* and as a patrimony derived from their forefathers.

Just so when the contest is with the foreign invaders of their rights, the panoply in which freemen arm themselves is the conviction that they have these rights. And the older their title, the better do they consider it, and the more they value and contend for it. The more it cost their fathers of struggling, and contest, and sacrifice, the more patiently will they endure in its defence the sacrifice of their substance, the more cheerfully the sacrifice of their lives.

Now, if it were proposed to plant a colony in Africa, selecting the colonists from the very best of our free coloured population, upon the theory and in the belief that in them has already taken place the requisite mental and moral developement; and if it were also proposed to give this colony, so carefully selected, at least one century to grow; it would, even then, be sufficiently doubtful (if history has taught mankind anything) whether, with all this care and pains, we could manufacture a republic on the African shore. But no such single and simple object, difficult as it would be of attainment, is proposed by the friends of African Colonization. The free negroes are a curse to this country, who must be got rid of. And therefore philanthropy is mightily stirred up by self-interest. Individual contributions, and the appropriations of the separate States, and biggest, and so best of all, those of the General Government, are to be united together; and at the same time, the most stringent legislature *here* against this unhappy class, and the most humane and benevolent treatment of them *there*, are to be called into operation, in the vain and delusive hope that without the needful mental and moral developement, without the needful progress of long ages of struggling and suffering and contest and discipline, a free and enlightened Republic can be constructed in Africa out of a set of wretches (to take the Society's own account of them) whom this continent cannot endure. " *Coelum non animum mutant qui trans mare currunt,*" was once true, but now a voyage across the ocean can make this "pestiferous class," this "degraded set," fit, and fit immediately, to rule the continent of Africa! Under the Society's auspices and by means merely of a voyage of thirty days, the poor, degraded, vicious negro will soon "blossom into something divine and beautiful :

> " And in another country, as they say,
> Bear a bright golden flower, but not in this soil."

"In some future stage of transatlantic being, they are to exhibit all the qualities of the negro, but improved and glorified :

> " 'Nothing of him that doth fade,
> But doth suffer a sea-change
> Into something rich and strange!' "

We are far from imputing selfishness to all the friends of African colonization; for, as we said above, it has undoubtedly enlisted the support of many of the purest and best men in this country. But there certainly is something absurd in this double aspect under which the scheme is often eloquently advocated. There is some quackery about this *nostrum* which promises by the simple efficacy of transportation from America to Africa, that it will transmit the greatest curse of the former into the greatest blessing of the latter.

We readily admit that a change of circumstances often produces the greatest effects on character. But the Colonization Society makes quite too much of this consideration. They either exaggerate the bad condition and character of the free negroes here, or else their good condition and character there. The mere passage across the Atlantic; the mere presence or absence of the white man, cannot produce such wondrous effects. The actual truth we suppose to be, that the change is favourable upon all that are not too low and degraded and ignorant, to be elevated and stimulated and improved by such a circumstance. But very many of those sent out are unquestionably incapable of feeling such beneficial effects. And therefore it is not fair to reason at all from their case in favour of the scheme. The whole argument, indeed, ought to run thus: There are a number of free blacks in the United States who are fit to go to the colony. It is a good thing for these persons, and for their families, and for Africa, and for their race everywhere, and for our race, too, that they be removed thither. Therefore let us help them to remove. And as for the miserable balance of them, let us bear the burden which a wise Providence has laid upon us, and redouble our efforts to do them good here, but let us never think of sending them to be a curse yonder! Or else let the argument run thus: It is better for us to remove all these free blacks to Africa. Therefore let us remove them, although it may be that they will degenerate, and even sink back into their original barbarism; for neither can we endure them here, nor they endure us; nor can we do them any good, nor they us; and so we have no use for them and they none for us, and let them begone!

Either of these lines of argument would be consistent and convincing. But the Colonization Society adopts neither. On the contrary, like most voluntary societies, that have to plead for patronage, they aim to enlist, as far as possible, all classes alike in their support. Accordingly, they argue that the free blacks are very bad here, but will be very good there. And their removal will be every way a very good thing. It will be good for the Southern master, by removing that class at the North most zealous in hindering the rendition of fugitive slaves; and good for the abolitionists, by constantly swelling the number of negroes emancipated from slavery. It will be good for the Northern cities, by ridding them of their domestic heathen, and good for the heathen of Africa, by tending to convert them to Christianity. It will work good, as against slavery, by growing cotton with free labour, and yet good, as on behalf of slavery, by sending away a class that we, slaveholders, ought to consider very dangerous. In fine, Liberia will afford us more and more, as she grows, a very good market for our goods, and at the same time, good riddance of our *bads*. And so the scheme is to bless both continents and all races, and is thus the fit harbinger of the reign of Universal Benevolence.

But the friends of this cause point us triumphantly to their colonies, where, they contend, we shall *see* the transmutation which they claim as within the potent influence of their scheme. And we do not deny, that in a certain degree they have thus far succeeded. But it does not appear to us that their success is nearly as great as they consider it. No one who reads the statements of the judicious writer whose book is our text, will say that the success of the colony is perfect. We quote a few of these statements:

"Trade is the chosen employment of the great mass of the Liberians." Page 406.

"The want of a disposition to cultivate the soil is, perhaps, the most discouraging feature in the prospects of Liberia." Page 407.

"The consequence is, that the community are still dependent upon this country and the industry of the aborigines around them, for the principal part of their provisions." Page 407.

"While there are individuals among them of intelligence and force of character enough to sustain themselves anywhere, the great mass of them, it cannot be denied, are too weak to withstand the influences of barbarism and superstition with which they must be surrounded in their new homes." Page 408.

"We regard it as one of the chief failings of the Liberians, and one of the most serious hinderances to their improvement, that they are too willing to be taken care of. They have no self-supporting schools; very little has been done to support the Gospel among themselves; and there is a disposition to look to the missionary societies to do everything of the kind for them; and the sooner they are *taught* to depend upon themselves the better." Page 410.

"The directors of the Colonization enterprise, we think, have erred in directing their efforts too exclusively to the one object of transporting emigrants to Liberia. Many regard the number actually sent out as the true, if not the only test of the prosperity of the enterprise. But this is a serious mistake, and if adhered to much longer, may prove the ruin of the cause." Page 410.

"Another great drawback to the prosperity of Liberia, is the undoubted unhealthiness of the climate, which, however, it is thought, is confined to the immediate sea-coast region. The process of acclimation must be passed through, even by coloured persons, and for the first six months it is quite as trying to them as it is to the whites. The only difference between the two is, that one may, after a certain time, become inured to the climate, while the other can scarcely ever become so." Page 411.

In addition to these statements of our author, we notice the fact of a recent attack by the natives upon one of the settlements, which was the cause of considerable loss of life, and great suffering. Also, that the Liberians are now anticipating great embarrassment for the want of food. The Rev. J. Burns, the superintendent of the Methodist mission in Western Africa, writes from Monrovia, under date of October 15, as follows:

"There is now a strong probability that the ensuing twelve months will be rather a serious time throughout Liberia for breadstuffs. This has been a very hard year, and produce of all kinds has been high. The misfortune is, that in many places, and for some weeks together, it could not be had for any price. Hundreds among the natives, even, have died of want. There is every reason to fear that the next year will be much worse than this."

Now, all this constitutes a somewhat darker picture of the state of things in Liberia than is usually given by its zealous friends. But were the true condition of the colonies ever so successful, up to this period, this circumstance is no adequate guarantee for its future prosperity. Because, for a few thousand blacks to be settled on the coast, most of them making a tolerable living by petty trading, (their chief support being from this country and from the natives,) is a small affair, compared with what is desired and expected by the Society. They have been almost from the first stronger than the petty kings of the country, and they have, for the most part, enjoyed the favour of some of the great powers of the earth. They have had help and protection from without, and no great dangers from within. Their very weakness taught them moderation and humanity, and preserved them from the machinations of the more ambitious among themselves. Meanwhile, no very difficult questions of external or internal policy have yet had to be settled among them. Above all, the friends of the colonies in the country have, up to a late period, been unwilling to suffer a too rapid increase of their members. The experiment has been, to some extent, cautiously carried on, and therefore it has not utterly failed. But within a few years past the Society has gained more strength at home. Several of the Northern States have made laws of the most stringent character against the settlement in their bounds of free blacks, and in favour, also, of their removal. In Ohio, the Constitutional Convention resolved, by a large majority, to let no negro or mulatto come into the State, to make all contracts with them void, and to fine all persons employing them not less than ten nor more than five hundred dollars. Indeed, nearly every State which has revised its constitution within twenty years, has made it more equal and democratic in respect to whites, and less so in res ect to the blacks. Besides all this legislation in favour of their end, the Society reported, in 1851, the bequest to them by John McDonough, of New Orleans, of twenty-five thousand dollars annually, for forty years; also, "the approach of *the good time* when we shall not be compelled to rely solely upon voluntary contributions to carry forward the work of colonization. The Legislature of Virginia has made a noble *beginning* in the work, by passing an act for the removal of free persons of colour to Liberia." P. 9. To carry this act into execution, the Legislature appropriated, for five years, thirty thousand dollars annually, besides taxes to the amount of fifteen thousand dollars annually. The

Society reported, moreover, at the same time, that similar action had nearly been taken in the Ohio Legislature, failing only for the want of time. Similar prospects in Indiana were opening, as also in Iowa, Kentucky, Missouri, Illinois, New Jersey, and New York. But the best part of the anticipated "good time" was referred to in the following words: "We also anticipate the action of the General Government in favor of colonization. From all parts of the country, the desire has been expressed that Congress should foster and encourage the work." P. 19. And then follows an account of the plan that was before Congress that year, 1851, for a line of steamers to run to Liberia, and convey emigrants to the colonies. "The colonization interest, therefore, in all parts of the country, (says the report,) is warmly in favour of the adoption of this scheme. The public press has almost universally come out in its favour, and advocated its adoption with great zeal and strong argument. It can hardly be doubted that the great ends to be accomplished present considerations of sufficient magnitude and importance to induce the government to adopt the measure. The suppression of the African slave-trade; the extension of American commerce; the opening of another market for American productions and manufactures; the elevation of a depressed race; the removal from our midst of an unfortunate class of people; the planting of civilization and Christianity on a foreign shore; and the redemption, from the deepest woes, of a whole continent; all combine and appeal to the honour, the benevolence, the patriotism and the justice of every true American, and urge the adoption of a policy which shall so rapidly advance one of the greatest glories of the age!" Turning to the report of the Committee on Naval Affairs, which recommended this plan to Congress, we find it contemplating the building by our government of "three steamships, of not less than four thousand tons burthen each, at a cost for each one, not to exceed nine hundred thousand dollars! The three vessels were to make altogether twelve voyages every year, and to convey, it was expected, fifteen hundred passengers at each voyage, making altogether eighteen thousand passengers yearly"! (See Report, pp. 24–28.) This report and this plan received the public sanction of Mr. Clay, in his speech quoted from, in the former part of this article. The occasion is described as having been a most "glorious" one. The "audience was immense." Mr. Clay himself presided. Mr. Fillmore, the President of the United States, sat at his right hand. The British Minister and the Russian Minister, with many Senators and Congress-men, were present. Mr. Clay endorsed this plan in the strongest terms; so did many other distinguished men. "Across that bridge of boats, (said one of these, speaking at the meeting,) there will go, with a tramp like an army with banners, a mighty crowd, whose Exodus will be more glorious than the Exodus of Israel."

If this effort, to engage by an unconstitutional act of Congress, the gigantic powers of the United States government in the service of the Colonization Society, failed, it was from no lack of zeal or energy on the part of that Society and its friends. They did what they could to accomplish this object. They regretted their failure to accomplish it. The directors and managers of the Society did not, in the year 1851, shrink from the idea of sending out eighteen thousand emigrants in one year, if so many could be tempted to go by the offer of a passage in a fine steamer, and if they could get the means from State appropriations to support them. No doubt they would still be willing to enlist this government in precisely such a plan. And we say, this disposition on the part of the Society and its friends constitutes a danger in the future, greater than any the colonies have yet passed through. No degree of success which may have attended the enterprise thus far, cautiously and slowly carried forward by the feeble hand of a voluntary association, can constitute any warrant for believing that its future success is at all certain, when its best friends have shown themselves capable of "killing it with kindness." Those pestiferous and degraded wretches whom America, free and enlightened and powerful America, cannot govern, cannot improve, and cannot endure, will ere long (if the Colonizationists can but have their way) be sent in crowds to poor Africa. Of those unhappy people, concerning whom Mr. Clay himself says that "they are more addicted to crime and vice, and dissolute manners, than any other portion of the people of the United States;" and that "the proportion of those who commit crimes and are sent to the penitentiary, of people of color, is infinitely greater than those of any other of the races that compose the aggregate of our population," (see page 38); of this wretched class of men, the capacious stomach of a steamer of four thousand tons is (if the Colonizationists can at any time carry their point) to disgorge itself upon the shores of weak and pitiable Liberia, of not less than fifteen hundred every month! The enrolment of eighty thousand Africans, as citizens of the Republic, was bad enough as an omen for the future prosperity of this unfortunate Republic. But worse would be the monthly prognostic of these mammoth steamships from the West, which a merciful Providence enabled the enemies of Colonization to hinder its friends from sending forth, for the ruin and destruction of these colonies.

We repeat, then, the fatal difficulty of the scheme in this aspect of it is, that it cannot be successful unless it can bring about two results which are absolutely incompatible with each other. It must *remove the free negroes rapidly*, or else it will not even keep pace with their natural increase, which is now about seven thousand annually. But it must at the same time remove *these same free negroes slowly*, or else the colony will be ruined by the too sudden influx of new comers; for the whole number of colonists, after thirty years operations, is now only about eight thousand, little more than the natural increase every year of the free blacks in America. The wheels of this Society, therefore, must *move fast* and they must *move slow* at one and the same time. Both objects aimed at, they can never accomplish, for they are completely incompatible. A black republic might grow up in Africa, if the best of the race only could be sent there, and sent slowly. But that is only one-half the object aimed at; and, moreover, that would require the refuse part of this population, which is much the larger part, to remain here. Such a pure philanthropy to Africa is, however, not generally claimed by the advocates of Colonization. They are anxious to send a blessing to Africa, but it is with the distinct understanding that we thereby rid ourselves of a curse!

Before quitting this branch of the subject, we make one further remark upon the connection of the white race at the North with this scheme. That connection, on the part of so many of the best men there, is a pregnant fact for us in our controversy as slaveholders. It is a most plain acknowledgement, even though unconsciously, of the righteousness of our position. If the free blacks at the North cannot be improved there, with all the training and kindness our brethren can bestow on them, it is plainly better that the unmanumitted mass, who cannot be removed, should be kept in slavery; for, as slaves in the midst of white men, they can and do improve. The friends of Colonization, therefore, whenever they dilate on the necessity of removing the free blacks, do thereby prove the righteousness of slavery. And never can a Colonizationist with any consistency favour the abolition or the weakening of the institution of slavery. If they find a few hundreds or thousands of free negroes so intolerable a burden, never should they be willing, for a moment, to have us burdened with millions of this population, in a condition of freedom for which they are not prepared. And yet, strangely enough, there are multitudes of good men at the North, friends of Colonization, in distinction from abolition, who do really in their hearts wish and expect and pray for the peaceful overthrow of our domestic institutions. There are many who have never considered our case as though it were their own; have never allowed the light of their own experience and observation to fall upon the case of their Southern brethren as it comes up before their minds, and who, therefore, wonder at the pertinacity with which we cling to that institution which forms the best relation for this population to sustain among us. Colonization, they consider the most glorious of schemes, because it rids them of the free blacks; but the emancipation of the black they consider next in glory to his Colonization, while slavery is evil and only evil. Yet the truth undoubtedly is, that whether Colonization be or be not what they represent it, slavery, in the circumstances, is undoubtedly good, and only good. We mean to say (and if any reader at the North should cast his eye on this page, we request him to notice carefully what we say,) that Slavery, so far from being, as they often represent it to be, the cause of negro indolence, ignorance, and licentiousness, has proved already, *in part*, the sure remedy of these evils; that while it is an evil to have three and one half millions of semi-barbarians existing anywhere, in the shape of men, yet, as they do exist in the midst of us, it is not *evil*, but *good* that they should stand in a relation to us by which we can govern, restrain, teach and improve them. If you choose, call the negro an evil, but the relation between that negro and his master is good. That relation has already changed the whole barbarian to a semi-barbarian. It is civilizing and christianizing him, that is, it affords *the occasion* of both these operations upon him. And we say, therefore, to the Colonization men at the North, whose ears, we suppose, are still open to the voice of their Southern brethren speaking for reason and for right, that what they would have us destroy is not only *not an evil*, but that it is the *only good there is* in the whole affair of negro existence in America. Without this relation, the case of both races would be indeed deplorable.

The second main ground on which the Colonization Society bases its title to favour has regard to the slave-trade. It sets up a very large claim for its colonies, as having put down and as keeping down this traffic. The naval affairs committee of the House of Representatives, in their report on the plan of steamers to Liberia, speak (page 15,) of its being "regarded, both in Europe and in this country, as a settled truth, that the planting and building up of Christian colonies on the coast of Africa is the only practical remedy for the slave-trade." And Mr. Clay, in his speech at the meeting referred to, said, "We have shown the most effectual and complete method, by which there can be an end put to that abominable traffic, and that is by Colonization." Now, there are two points involved in this claim of the Society; first, whether the traffic has been put down; and secondly, whether the colonies have done this work. We have testimony to produce on both points, but before we proceed to introduce it, we must take occasion very frankly to express our judgement upon the reopening of the slave-trade; a measure recommended in his message to the Legislature by the late highly respected chief magistrate of this Commonwealth, and by them referred to a special committee, with leave to sit during the recess, and to report at the next session. We hesitate not to avow that, in every aspect of the case, we are opposed to the measure. We regret the very agitation of the subject, for while it can do no good, it may do harm. We could not, if we would, reopen the trade. The agitation of the subject will tend to divide South Carolina within herself. It will also tend to divide the South, of late more united than formerly, and the complete union of which, in her own defence, is all important.

But we have overwhelming objections to the measure itself. In the first place, it would change the whole character of the relation as it exists amongst us. *Now*, it is domestic and patriarchal; the slave has all the family pride and sympathies of the master. He is born in the house and bred with the children. The sentiments which spring from this circumstance, in both master and slave, soften all the asperities of the relation. They secure obedience on the part of the slave as a sort of filial respect. They secure kindness and sympathy on the part of the master as a kind of paternal affection. All these humanizing elements would be lost the moment we cease to rear our slaves and rely upon a foreign market. Pitt, in his splendid speech on the abolition of the slave trade, proved, upon data furnished by the West India planters themselves, that the moment an end was put to the slave trade, the natural increase of the negroes would commence, but that otherwise there could be no such increase.* The reason was, that so long as the slave was made cheap by the trade, the master's pecuniary interest was more operative than his sympathies. In Brazil now, (as in Louisiana before her annexation,) it costs less to buy an adult negro from Africa than to rear an infant. We do not want to see the day come amongst us when it will be economy to wear out our negroes and buy new ones, rather than to take care of them and of their increase. But, *in the next place*, the reopening of this traffic would render the institution positively dangerous. Lawless savages, imported from Africa, many of whom have been accustomed to command, to war, and to cruelty, and none of whom have been accustomed to work, would be the surest instruments of insubordination and rebellion that could be devised. We should have to resort to a standing army, as they do in the West Indies, to keep our plantations in order. It suited our fathers to take such savages and tame them, because our fathers were the pioneers of this country, but it would not suit our generation, softened, as we have been, by long years of ease, and safety, and prosperity; or if it would suit any of this generation, it would be only those who have gone, and do go out into the South-western wilderness to subdue its roughness by their hardy vigour. *In the third place*, the whole scheme proceeds on a blunder. Capital and labour, with us, are not distinct. The slave is as really capital as he is a labourer. To reduce his value, therefore, is not simply to cheapen labour, it is also to diminish capital. The country will be no richer by the foreign importation. To show how a great and wise political economist of Virginia, who profoundly studied this question, judged very differently of its pecuniary bearings from those who are now urging the reopening of the slave-trade, we quote the following sentence from Professor Dew's Essay on Slavery:

* See Dew on Slavery, page 371.

5

"Perhaps one of the greatest blessings (if it could be reconciled to our conscience) which could be conferred on the Southern portion of the Union, would arise from the total abolition of the African slave-trade and the opening of the West India and British American markets to our slaves."

His idea is for the South to grow rich, not by the importation of new slaves, but by a new and constant market for those she has to spare from time to time, at their full value. But we are free to admit the difficulty of judging what would be the effect of reopening this trade upon the pecuniary prosperity of the South. It might operate differently from what we have supposed, and so also it might operate differently from what its advocates suppose. Perhaps the reopening of this trade, while it might remove our present difficulty, viz: the scarcity of slave labour, faster than their natural increase can do this, would expose us to the very opposite embarrassment, viz: a redundancy of the labouring population, which is an evil Europe has laboured under for centuries. Perhaps, as was urged by Mr. Cochran, of Alabama, in the late Commercial Convention at Savannah, to deprive ourselves of an outlet for that redundancy of our slave labour which must be produced in the old States in a few years, by filling up the new countries of the South-west with labourers imported now from Africa, might prove to be bad policy. The question, in these pecuniary and political aspects of it, is vast and complicated, and may well baffle human sagacity, and multiply the speculations of political economists. There is one aspect of the question, however, that is perfectly plain; and this forms our fourth and *last ground* of objection to reopening this traffic. It is an immoral traffic. If you reopen the trade, you will not only *buy slaves* in Africa, but you (that is, your agents) will go there and *steal men;* and while the Bible allows the one, it condemns the other. It is nothing to the purpose to say (what is, doubtless, true enough) that it is, after all, for the benefit and advantage of these very men to be stolen. We may not "do evil that good may come." The South can afford a great pecuniary loss; she can afford a political weakness or deficiency; but she cannot afford to *put the Bible against her.* She cannot afford to sanction an immoral traffic. You might regulate the traffic after it reaches our shores; you might even reform the "*middle passage*"; but you could not regulate the trade, as it would operate in Africa. There, it would be the fruitful cause of wars, and bloodshed and seditions, and man-stealing. Professor Dew observes, that "wars in Africa have been made more mild by the trade, yet they have been made much more frequent. An additional and powerful motive for strife has been furnished. Countries have been overrun, and cities pillaged, mainly with a view of procuring slaves for the slave-dealer." "Brougham (he says) likens the operation of the slave-trade, in this respect, to the effect which the different menageries in the world, and the consequent demand for wild beasts, have produced on the inferior animals of Africa. They are now taken alive, instead of being killed, as formerly; but they are certainly more hunted and more harassed than if no foreign demand existed for them."

At the risk of making this digression too long, we would here observe, ere we quit this subject, that, in our view, his Excellency the late Governor's argument was a *non sequitur*, when he said: "If the slave-trade be piracy, then slaves are plunder." It is evident that the Bible distinguishes between slavery as an existing institution and the "stealing of men," which, of course, shows, and on the highest authority, that we are not to confound them. And, moreover, it seems to us plain that, while any criminal act by which a man is reduced to bondage, (for there are ways, undoubtedly, of his being so reduced that are not criminal,) " can never come to be otherwise than criminal, yet the relations to which that act gave rise may themselves be consistent with the will of God, and the foundation of new and important duties. The relations of a man to his natural offspring, though wickedly formed, give rise to duties which would be ill discharged by the destruction of the child." Plunder, the forefathers of our slaves undoubtedly were, if stolen, and not born slaves in Africa; but our slaves themselves, as born in slavery, are not plunder. The true and only title of any man to liberty, as of property, is *inheritance*, or *honest and legal acquisition*, both of which depend upon the discriminations of Providence, and not upon any abstract natural equality. The legal maxim is just and right—*Partus sequitur ventrem*—that is, all men have an equal and perfect right to the *status* in which they are born, with all its established rights and privileges, and also to whatever else they can legally and meritoriously acquire. Some men are rulers, some subjects; some are rich, some poor; some are fathers, some children; some are bond, some free. And if a man is justly and providentially a ruler, he has the rights of a ruler; if a husband, the rights of a husband; if a father, the rights of a father; and if a slave, only the rights of a slave.

We now beg the patient reader to go back with us to the points we left, viz: Has the slave-trade been put down? and, Have the colonies on the coast put it down?

As to the first point, we read of late, almost daily, in the newspapers, of vessels being fitted out at the North to carry on this trade. Here is a paragraph on the subject from a very respectable sheet in New York—the "Journal of Commerce"—of December 11, 1856:

"THE SLAVE TRADE FLOURISHING.—A gentleman who has recently arrived in this city, from the coast of Africa, states that he learned from good authority that there were thirty vessels, principally Portuguese, or sailing under that character, lying in the creeks at the mouth of the Congo river, waiting for cargoes of slaves, and on the look-out for opportunities to get to sea unperceived by the cruisers. Sheltered by the thick growth of forest which abounds there, these slavers are safe from observation. Persons are stationed near the mouth of the river to give warning of the vicinity of national vessels, and when the coast is clear, the traders select a dark night and a fair wind, and effect their escape in safety. The English government have a steamer on the coast, but it is too slow to be of much service. With a propitious breeze, the smart clipper-built slavers find little difficulty in evading the pursuit of their clumsy antagonist. Not long ago, a brig (supposed to be an American craft) was making her way out of the mouth of the Congo river, with four hundred negroes on board, when she was espied by the steamer, which promptly gave chase. The brig slipped away from her pursuer with the greatest ease; the steamer fired several shots at her, but without success. When the brig had got out of the reach of the steamer's guns, the captain, by way of tantalizing the cruizer, ordered a negro to be pulled up to the yard-arm, where he was allowed to hang for some time, as an insulting token of the acknowledged character of the vessel. The captain also signified his exultation by standing at the stern and fiddling as his brig scudded away. It is said that the trade in the vicinity of the Congo might be stopped, or at least materially diminished, by a small well-armed steamer, capable of sailing fourteen miles an hour, which should cruise at intervals for a short distance up and down the river."

In the late Commercial Convention at Savannah, Mr. Gaulden, (Goulding?) of Georgia, is reported to have stated that England had withdrawn her squadron from the coast. This we suppose is not strictly correct. She has not maintained it in the state of efficiency which it had attained before the beginning of the Russian war, but she will doubtless now reinforce it. Mr. Wilson's opinion is, that "occasional cargoes of slaves are still carried off from that coast, especially since the partial withdrawal of the squadron on account of the Eastern war, but the system by which it was carried on so extensively in former times is broken up." He says : "From Senegal to Cape Lopez, a distance of something like two thousand five hundred miles, there is now, with the exception of three factories, on what is called the Slave Coast, no trade in slaves whatever. In fact, the trade, with these exceptions, is now confined to what is called the Congo country, in which there are not more than eight or ten points where slaves are collected, and from whence they are shipped. If we add to these the three above mentioned, we have, on the whole, not more than twelve or fourteen, whereas there were, even within the knowledge of the writer, nearly four times this number." P. 435. Yet Mr. Wilson admits that it may be objected, "although the trade has been shut up to fewer points, the only consequence is, that it is carried on more vigorously at these, and that the number still exported is as great as it ever was." And in replying to this objection, we find him employing no stronger language than this, that in reference to the force of it, he has "more than his doubts." And he proceeds to argue that nothing can be known, positively, on the subject. "The time has been when tolerably accurate statistics might be collected on this subject, but we do not see how this can be done at present. There is no one on the coast of Africa who can furnish anything like accurate information; and as most of the slaves which reach Brazil are smuggled into places where there is the least likelihood of their being detected, we doubt whether there is any one there that can furnish information upon which more reliance can be placed." P. 437. And he adds: "Our own impression is, that the number of slaves exported has vastly diminished." This is all which Mr. Wilson (as good authority as is to be found) can give us on this subject; he gives us his impressions, but he asserts nothing.

We have produced testimony enough, we think, to show that it is not so certain as the Colonization Society and its friends represent, that the slave trade has been put down.

But, admitting, as we must do, that the slave-trade has been driven away from many parts of the coast, is it true, as the Society maintains, that their colonies have been the authors of this? Mr. Wilson says: "It is unquestionably true that important aid has been derived from these settlements in breaking up the slave-factories in their immediate vicinity, but it is equally true that they could have rendered no such aid had it not been for the countenance and support which they received from the English and other men-of-war on the coast. And for the simple reason, that none of these settlements, nor all of them together, have sufficient naval force to contend with a single armed slaver. If they have it in their power to destroy any barracoons that may be established in their immediate neighbourhood, by marching a land force against them, their enemies, if not intimidated by the presence of so many men-of-war, could at any time take ample revenge by destroying what little commerce they have, if they did not put in imminent peril the most promising settlements on the coast." Page 437. He says, also, that these settlements "have always had and still need the protection of foreign governments. There are few, if any of them, that could withstand the combination of hostile natives that would be formed against them, especially when they were instigated and supported by Spanish and Portuguese slave-traders." "Those who have allowed themselves to be persuaded that they have already acquired sufficient strength to protect themselves, or who depend on them to do anything effective in putting down the slave-trade without the coöperation of the squadron, will find out, ere long, that they have leaned upon a broken reed." Page 444.

We think Mr. Wilson's sober statements make it plain that there has been very great exaggeration employed by Colonization orators, in setting forth the influence and power, as against the slave-trade, of a few thousand coloured people that occupy some little spots on that extensive coast.

But let us pass on to the third main ground on which the society sets its claim to favour and support, which is, that it is really a Christian Missionary scheme. With the good Christian people of our country this is really, after all, the great argument for African Colonization, and, we think that of late, it is the one most earnestly presented by its advocates generally. It is indeed strange, when men of all sorts—orators of all kinds of personal character and religious ideas—are found uniting in such an ardent advocacy of the missionary cause. One would think that the world had fallen in love with Christianity, and that missions to the heathen are not generally viewed with a secret and real contempt, obliging us to make an apologetic defence of that cause in the first part of this article. We have quoted a few specimens of the manner in which this religious aspect of the case has been presented; not designing to insinuate, however, that in these particular cases there is any inconsistency in such a testimony from such parties.

The Hon. Elisha Whittlesey says:

"Every intelligent emigrant from this country is a missionary to and an instructor of his brethren. Africa will be Christianized when parts of Asia will be in heathen darkness."

The Maryland Colonization Journal says:

"Every argument which can be adduced to prove that it is both lawful and expedient to send men out to labour for the evangelization of the world, in any of the departments of the Christian Church, may be used in its measure to prove that the cause of African Colonization possesses claims to a position side by side with them. Is the Bible so good, so heavenly in its mission, that the best divines of our day, and of other years, hesitate not to become its advocates and agents? Colonization is the best colporteur that cause ever had. Is the great missionary enterprise held in such estimation in the eye of the Church, that men of the first talents and most gigantic intellect are willing to deny themselves the endearments of home, and go in person to lands of barbarism and most repulsive degradation and vice, to 'preach the truth as it is in Jesus?' Were such men as Heber and Judson, Phillips and Williams, with a noble army from other lands and this, willing to go? Colonization is a missionary society *by wholesale*, and eternity only will develope how much it has had to do with the heralds of salvation in the redemption of Africa."

Matthew St. Clair Clarke, Esq., of Washington, says:

"It is the only means which, under the blessing of God, can bring light out of gloom, order out of disorder, mind out of instinct, civilization out of barbarism, and heaven-born truth out of pagan superstition and cruelty."

The Rev. James A. Lyon, Pastor of the Westminster (Presbyterian) Church, St. Louis, says:

"Here, then, is the 'salt' that is to redeem Africa from her impurities and corruptions—here is the 'leaven' that is to convert the multitudinous nations of that continent into a homogeneous brotherhood; and here is the 'light' that is to penetrate all the dark places of that benighted land, and dissipate ignorance, superstition, and degrading error."

The Naval Committee of the House of Representatives say:

"These colonies will be the means, at no distant period, of disseminating civilization and Christianity throughout the whole of that continent. As a missionary enterprise, therefore, the colonization of Africa by the descendants of Africans on this continent deserves, and no doubt will receive, the countenance and support of the whole Christian world." Report, p. 14.

And Mr. Clay, in a speech before the Society, January 18, 1848, said:

"What Christian is there who does not feel a deep interest in sending forth missionaries to convert the dark heathen, and bring them within the pale of Christianity? But what missionaries can be so potent as those it is our purpose to transport to the shores of Africa? Africans themselves by birth, or sharing at least African blood, will not all their feelings, all their best affections, induce them to seek the good of their countrymen? At this moment there are four or five thousand colonists who have been sent to Africa under the care of this Society; and I will venture to say that they will accomplish, as missionaries of the Christian religion, more to disseminate its blessings than *all the rest of the missionaries throughout the world.*" Report, p. 61.

Now, with all respect for those who entertain this idea of the necessary operation of the colonies, we must say that we have no belief at all in the evangelization of Africa by any such means. And after much reading and reflection upon the subject of colonization, and long observation, too, of the operation of Christian Missions, we say deliberately that we regard this aspect of the scheme of Colonization as its weakest and most unreal aspect.

We suppose that one especial occasion of this opinion is the belief which has arisen, that white men cannot live in Africa; and that, consequently, if Africa is to be evangelized at all, it must be by negroes. And at the same time, benevolent hearts, looking to find some explanation of the permission given in God's providence for the introduction, by so much violence and so much suffering, of slaves and slavery on this continent, have eagerly seized upon this opinion as the explanation of this mystery. Now, we are not of those who see mystery in any of the movements of Providence, once it is admitted that sin is in this world by God's permission.

That is *the mystery*. After that, nothing which men suffer here is mysterious. But if a solution of slavery in this aspect of it must be had, it is surely enough of explanation when we see thousands of these African slaves admitted into the Christian Church all through the South. It is not necessary to the vindication of God's ways to man, supposing man could without presumption undertake such a vindication, that we should say the evangelization of Africa is to grow out of slavery. If there grow out of it the civilizing and Christianizing our slaves, that is vindication enough. But is it not presumption for us to say that Africa cannot be evangelized except by blacks? Is the Divine Author of Christian Missions limited in power, so that he cannot take care of white men who go to carry thither His Word? Or supposing that Africa is to be the grave-yard of the European, American, or Asiatic races, as often as they may in humble faith undertake to avangelize Africa; supposing this is appointed to be so, we ask is the difficulty of sickly or deadly climates the only difficulty in that work of converting the world which has been undertaken by our Omnipotent Captain?

In point of fact, we do not believe the allegation that the white man cannot live in Africa. Mr. Wilson, who lived there himself eighteen years, expresses the opinion that the danger has been greatly magnified, is common to negro and to white men, is peculiar to certain localities, and is greatly attributable to that want of experience which always endangers the stranger in a strange land. He says:

"Commander Chamberlain of Her Britannic Majesty's brig *Britomart*, informed the writer that he had been cruising on the coast nearly two years, without having lost a man, or having had, so far as he knew, a single case of African fever on board his vessel; the United States sloop of war *Yorktown*, with a crew of nearly two hundred men, cruised on the coast two years without having lost a single man; and the writer was informed by Capt. Bell, that he had never had a healthier crew in any part of the world." Page 449.

He tells us "there are not less than three thousand whites now living on that coast and on the Islands adjacent; and that if you add to this the floating population engaged in commerce and the suppression of the slave-trade, the whole white population cannot be less than six or eight thousand." "And we may add to all this, that there is a considerable number of individuals of affluence, who reside in that country as a matter of preference." Page 522.

" On this subject, I have no convictions I would wish to conceal. The insalubrity of the climate has been, and I presume ever will be, to a greater or less extent, a serious hinderance to the progress of the Gospel in Western Africa; and this difficulty exists, be it known, irrespective of the kind of agency that may be employed in carrying it on. For the *coloured man* from these United States is as sure to feel the effects of the climate as *the white man;* and if the physical constitution of the former possesses some advantage in adapting itself more readily to the climate, I am not sure but the other will have equally as much advantage in his superior discretion and the precautionary measures which he will practice to preserve his health. The difficulty in either case, however, has been unduly magnified." Page 511.

"The Christian public in this country has had no means of forming a judgment on the subject, except by the number of deaths that have occurred among their missionaries; and these have been paraded before the public mind by the opposers of African Missions with such studied care, that no one case has failed to produce its full effect."

"Now, while no one can be more sensible than ourselves of the extent and severity of these losses, we feel that it has been specially unfortunate for the cause of truth and humanity, that the attendant circumstances and collateral causes of most of these calamities have not been made equally prominent at the same time."

"And *first*, there are certain points along the coast of Africa, as in all other countries, that, by local causes, have been rendered more unhealthy than the country generally. Of these, none are supposed to be more so than Sierra Leone and Cape Messurado. I do not remember ever to have heard a dissent from this opinion by a single individual whose judgment was entitled to respect; and yet it is from statistics of sickness and mortality that have occurred at these two places, chiefly, that the public, both in England and America, have derived their impressions of the unhealthiness of the country at large."

"But there are other and still weightier considerations."

"I allude to the peculiar difficulties and trials in which most of the missions to Africa have had their origin."

"It will be borne in mind, that all of them, except those of Sierra Leone and Gambia, have been founded within the last twenty-five years. The places selected for most of these were not only new and unbroken ground, so far as all missionary influence was concerned, but many of them were located in the bosom of heathen tribes, who had scarcely any intercourse with the civilized world. Most of the missionaries were pioneers in a difficult undertaking. They were unfurnished with missionary experience, and in many instances, they were without the aid of Christian counsel. They found themselves, at the commencement of their labours, among a people who could not comprehend the object of their mission, and who regarded all their professions of friendship and disinterestedness with distrust. They were ignorant of the native character, and it required much labour to master their barbarous languages, through which alone they could arrive at correct knowledge of their character, or hope to influence their minds. In many instances, they were without medical aid, and in others, when physicians were at hand, those physicians themselves were inexperienced in the treatment of African diseases; and in every instance, the missionaries were pressed down by the cares, anxieties, and responsibilities incident to all new misions. So that, when all these things are taken into the account, we almost wonder that the mortality has not been greater; we almost marvel that any have escaped."

"But this perilous crisis, we believe, has been passed. The most formidable obstacles have been removed, and the missionary work, it is believed, will henceforth move forward more easily and with less sacrifice of life. Missionaries in that country, notwithstanding their losses, their reverses, their afflictions and bereavements, have been sustained in their work, and obtained a firm footing on many points along that coast. A large amount of missionary experience has been acquired: the roughness of native character has been smoothed down; the habits, customs, and feelings of the natives are better understood by the missionaries; and the objects of the missionaries are better understood by the natives. Many of the most difficult dialects of the country have been reduced to writing, and now serve, not only as easy and direct channels of conveying religious truth to the minds of the people, but will serve as a clue to the acquisition of all other languages in the country. Missionaries going to that country hereafter, will find missionary brethren on the ground to welcome them and give them all needed counsel and aid. In this way they will escape much of the wasting care and anxieties that were unavoidable at the commencement of this undertaking. They may now go to Africa with the reasonable prospect of *living;* and if they cannot calculate upon enjoying the same amount of vigorous and elastic health that they would in their native country, they may at least expect to have strength enough to proclaim the unsearchable riches of the Gospel to thousands of their fellow-men who are perishing for the want of it. There is a reasonable prospect that white missionaries, provided they are endowed with the faith, the courage and the perseverance befitting their high calling, may live in that country to establish Christian churches there, which will be able, in due time, not only to sustain themselves, but to communicate their blessings to the remotest region of that benighted continent. This is all we can promise. This is the view of the subject upon which we base our arguments. We believe no obstacles lie in the way of this undertaking as thus stated, except such as have been permitted by God, to try the faith and courage of his people. The bare existence of trials and difficulties, provided they are not insuperable, is never a sufficient cause for abandoning any great and good undertaking. No great result, fraught with blessings to mankind, has ever been achieved in this apostate world of ours, except by a triumph of patient perseverance over difficulties and discouragements. Human probabilities have always been arrayed against the promises of the Bible; and if missionaries were to look at the former, without regard to the latter, every field of missionary labour would have been abandoned long ere this."—Pages 512–15.

There is another prevalent idea, having reference to *the Natives of Africa,* which has contributed to create the opinion we are considering, viz: the idea that the aborigines of Africa are so turbulent and savage in their habits that no missionary could live among them, except so far as he might enjoy the countenance and protection of some civilized power which the natives would hold in fear. On this subject, we quote from Mr. Wilson, not only to show how little weight is due to such an objection to white missions in Africa, (an objection by the way, which would apply equally to black ones) but also to exhibit to our readers, the nobleness of character, and of feelings, and of behaviour, which go to make up the true Missionary of the cross.

"It (this current idea) has its origin in such low views of the nature and power of the Gospel; it so dishonours the promise of the Saviour to be with his disciples to the end of the world, and is so completely refuted by the history of missions in almost every portion of the habitable world, that it might safely be thrust aside as an argument unworthy of serious consideration."

"It is, in reality, but the revival of that oft-refuted idea, that civilization must precede Christianity in reclaiming the heathen tribes of the earth; and the argument is specially unfortunate when applied to Africa, inasmuch as her history furnishes many of the most striking illustrations of the utter impotency of all secular power to benefit a heathen people. And while there is no set of men in the world whose situation and circumstances naturally lead them to set a higher value upon the blessings of enlightened governments than the missionaries of the cross, in the majority of cases, nevertheless, they find themselves in circumstances where duty to the heathen compels them to protest against the measures and designs of these very governments."

"But, apart from all speculation, what is there, it may be asked, in the history of missions in Western Africa, to warrant the opinion under consideration."

"No one who has given attention to the subject, can be ignorant of the fact that, of the numerous missionary stations established in that country during the last fifteen years, the majority of them are located, not only beyond the jurisdiction of all civil governments, but many of them in situations where no civilized government on earth could render them aid, however urgent might be their distress."

"And yet we ask, what one of those stations has been cut off by native violence? What spot of African soil has been stained with the blood of these missionaries? Is there an individual in whose mind are not called up associations of unparalleled cruelty in connection with the names of Ashanti, Dehomi, Badagry, and Kalibar? And yet in these dark abodes of cruelty, Christian missions have been planted; the Gospel is statedly preached; missionaries live in peace and security, and pursue their work with a confident assurance that, ere long even these dark habitations will be filled with the light and blessings of the Gospel."

"As there seems to be a general misapprehension in relation to native character, as found in Africa, I may be excused for introducing personal experience in illustration of the subject."

"During my residence in that country, I have traveled many thousands of miles among these people, sometimes on water and sometimes by land, among tribes to whom I was known, and among those who had never seen a white man. I have gone among them in times of peace and in times of war. I have visited them at their homes, and I have met them on their way to shed the blood of their fellow-men. And yet, in all these journeyings among remote, and to me, unknown tribes, I never thought it necessary to furnish myself with a single implement of defence, nor was I ever placed in circumstances where there would have been any just cause for using such a weapon, even if I had been supplied."

"Among those of the natives to whom I was known as a Minister of the living God, I have generally traveled alone; and on many occasions when called upon to visit the sick, or to perform some other errand of mercy, I have passed through the largest villages alone and in the middle of the night, with a feeling of as much security as I could possibly have felt in traversing the streets of any city in these United States, under similar circumstances. And so far from finding it impossible to live among them, I may further add, that during the whole term of my residence in that country, I scarcely remember to have heard a single syllable from the lips of one of these people which could, in any just sense, be construed as an intentional insult to myself."

" It is far from my intention to leave the impression, that the natives of Africa are perfectly inoffensive in their habits. They are *heathen* in the full sense of that word, and no missionary can live among them without finding ample cause of perplexity and annoyance. But when it is affirmed that the missionary cannot live among them on account of their turbulence and lawlessness, the assertion is without foundation." Pages 509–11.

It is not true, then, either that the climate or the natives of Africa are such as to make it indispensable that her heathen tribes be furnished with the gospel only by black men. And as to their being no hope of their evangelization except from the colonies of Liberia, we say, the pretence is perfectly contrary to all history, and to the Bible.

It has, indeed, been asserted by an authority which we esteem very high, that "Europe became what she is by colonization, and by this, America was christianized," and that " colonization has been, in past ages, the great and glorious plan of missions." But we think a great, and wise, and good man never made a greater error. We assert, unhesitatingly, on the contrary, that from the beginning, Christianity has been propagated by Missionaries in distinction from Colonists. We have tried, in vain, to recall a single instance recorded in Ecclesiastical history, ancient or modern, in which colonization has established the gospel among a heathen people. America was, indeed, christianized by colonies, but the aboriginal inhabitants of America were not so christianized. The colonists took the soil of America and christianized it, in the sense of growing up upon it into a great and mighty Christian nation, but they exterminated the Indians that dwelt upon it formerly. And as to Europe, it was Missionaries that converted her as well as Asia, and it is Missionaries that are, by God's blessing, to convert Africa.

Any respectable work on Ecclesiastical History will verify our assertions. The Book of the Acts tells us that the Apostles carried the gospel in that early day to nations near and remote. " Eusebius tells us that in the second century Pantænus carried it *to the Indians*, by which may be meant either the Persians, Parthians, Medes, Arabians, Ethiopians, or Lybians. Jerome thought it was those we now call East Indians, for he represents him as sent to instruct the Brahmins." In the second century, we first find unequivocal proofs of the existence of churches in Transalpine Gaul, now called France. But who planted them? History tells us it was Pothinus, "a man of distinguished piety and devotedness to Christ, in company with Irenaeus and other holy men, who proceeded from Asia to Gaul, and there instructed the people with such success that he gathered churches of Christians at Lyons and Vienne, of which Pothinus himself was the first Bishop." Eminent French writers have, indeed, disputed about the precise origin of their churches, but none of them pretend to say that colonies brought the gospel to Gaul—it was *these* Missionaries, or it was *those* missionaries.

In the third century, "the Goths, a ferocious and warlike people that inhabited Mœsia and Thrace, and made perpetual incursions into the neighbouring provinces, received a knowledge of Christ from certain Priests whom they carried captive from Asia. Philostorgius says it was the influence of the Christian captives which induced the Goths to invite Christian teachers among them." But whether the one account or the other be correct, it was still, in either case, individual teaching and testifying which converted those Goths.

In the fourth century, "Gregory first persuaded private individuals in Armenia, afterwards the King Tiridates, and finally the Nobles to embrace Christianity, and for thus driving away the mists of superstition from their minds, this missionary was called 'the Illuminator.' It was he who gradually spread Christianity throughout that country." "In the middle of this century, Frumentius proceeded from Egypt into Abyssinia, and baptized the king and many of the nobles." "To the Georgians, a Christian woman, who had been carried captive thither, was the first missionary. She persuaded them to send for other teachers to Constantinople."

Hitherto, we read of no conversions to Christianity, except through the teachings of missionaries. But we are descending far from the pure fountain head, and the stream begins to be muddy. We have just been reading of a part of the Goths converted by their captives. Now we hear of Constantine the Great "vanquishing them and the Sarmatians, and engaging great numbers of them to become Christians." Whether he "engaged" them to this change by the mere effect of the vanquishing, or whether he brought them over by teaching, we are not told; but it is plain that colonization was not the means of their conversion. "But still, a large part of the nation remained (says Mosheim,) estranged from Christ until the time of the Emperor Valens, who permitted them to pass the Danube and inhabit Dacia, &c. on condition that they would be subject to the Roman laws and embrace Christianity, to which condition their king Fritigern consented." They were *bought* to be Christians by the Emperor Valens, and they were probably just about such Christians as Constantine "engaged" the others to be, when he vanquished them. Mosheim remarks, that in this century whole nations as well as individuals found cogent reasons for embracing Christianity in the fear of the Roman arms, and the desire of pleasing the Emperor. " Yet (says he) no person well informed in the history of this period, will ascribe the extension of Christianity wholly to these causes. For it is manifest that the untiring zeal of the bishops and other holy men, the pure and devout lives which many of the Christians exhibited, the translations of the sacred volume, and the excellence of the Christian religion, were as efficient motives with many persons, as the arguments from worldly advantage and disadvantage were with others." Nothing is said of colonies in this century as the means of spreading Christianity. But special mention is made of " the great Martin, Bishop of Tours, who travelled through the provinces of Gaul; persuaded many to renounce their idols and embrace Christianity; destroyed their temples and threw down their statues; and who therefore, deserved the title of the *Apostle of the Gauls.*" He was evidently a great *missionary.*

In the fifth century we find a still muddier stream. "The German nations who rent in pieces the Western Roman Empire were either Christians before that event or they embraced Christianity after establishing their kingdoms, in order to reign more securely among the Christians. But at what time, and by whose instrumentality the Vandals, the Suevi, the Alans, and some others, became Christians, is still uncertain, and is likely to remain so. As to the Burgundians who dwelt along the Rhine, and thence passed into Gaul, it appears from Socrates that they voluntarily became Christians, near the commencement of the century. Their motive to this step was the hope that Christ, or the God of the Romans, who they were informed was immensely powerful, would protect them from the incursions and ravages of the Huns. They afterwards joined the Arian party, to which also the Vandals, Suevi, and Goths, were addicted."

In this century Clovis or Lewis, king of the Franks, " when in a desperate situation in battle with the Allemanni implored the aid of Christ, and vowed to worship him as God, if he gained the victory. He did conquer, and stood to his promises, and was baptized at Rheims; some thousands of Franks followed his example." But in his case, we read of something better than existed in the case of the Germans. He had " a wife, Clotildis, a Christian, and she had long recommended Christ to him in vain." She was the Missionary, and planted the seed in his mind which at last germinated.

In this century also, we read of Succathus, a Scotchman, whose name was changed to Patricius (Patrick) who converted many of the Irish to Christianity. He was " the Apostle of Ireland," that is, its missionary.

Mosheim very properly comments upon the mixture of motives which operated with many in this century, to abandon their false gods and profess Christianity. There is not a word however, about colonization as the means of any of them being, either "soundly" or "unsoundly" converted.

In the sixth century we are told that "Gregory the Great, sent forty Benedictine Monks into Britain, with Augustine at their head, to complete the work which Bertha, wife of Ethelbert, King of Kent, had begun to accomplish, partly by her own influence and partly by that of the ministers of religion whom she had brought with her from Paris." By this double missionary effort, the King and the people of Kent were converted.

The seventh century witnessed various missionary labours among the Gauls, the Franks, and other nations of the West, and also the splendid success of the Nestorians of the East, who, " with incredible industry and perseverance, laboured to propagate the Gospel from Syria and India, among the barbarous and savage nations inhabiting the deserts and the remotest shores of Asia. And that their zeal was not inefficient, appears from numerous proofs still existing. In particular, the vast empire of China was, by their zeal and industry, enlightened with the light of Christianity."

In the eighth century we still read of Christianity being disseminated in the remote East by the Nestorians. In Europe, Boniface was famous as a missionary, and was called "The Apostle of Germany." So was Corbinian, and so too, was Pirmin, a French Monk, and so was Lebwin, an English one. They were, doubtless, not missionaries of an uncorrupted Christianity, yet they were spreading their doctrines by individual persuasions and arguments and influence. Charlemagne in this century, sought to convert the Saxons by force of arms, joined to rewards, and at length succeeded.

We should wear out the patience of our readers were we to pursue this investigation all down through the dark ages. The result however, would be still the same; constant endeavours amidst all the superstition of the times to propagate opinions, and always by the missionary in distinction from the colonist! Even where the power of Kings and armies is employed, still it is in connection with teachers *individually engaged in propagating opinions*, and never by colonies sent out for that purpose. Coming down to the sixteenth century, when the Reformation took place, we read, that " the Roman Pontiffs, after losing a great part of Europe, were roused to new zeal to propagate Christianity in other parts of the world. For no better method occurred to them, both for repairing the loss they had sustained in Europe, and for vindicating their claims to the title of common fathers of the Christian Church. Therefore, soon after the institution of the celebrated society of Jesuits, in the year 1540, they were especially charged constantly to train up suitable men, to be commissioned, and sent by the Pontiffs into the remotest regions as preachers of the religion of Christ. With what fidelity and zeal the order obeyed their injunction, may be learned from the long list of histories which describe the labours and perils encountered by vast numbers of the fraternity, while propagating Christianity among the pagan nations." Mosheim's Ecclesiastical History, iii, 84.

In the seventeenth century, (1622,) was established at Rome, the famous "Congregatio de propaganda fide." Then in 1627, also at Rome, "the College or Seminary for propagating the faith," and in 1663 in France, "the Congregation of Priests for Foreign Missions," and likewise the "Parisian Seminary for Missions to Foreign Nations." From these colleges and societies (says Mosheim) issued those swarms of missionaries who travelled over the whole world, so far as it is yet discovered, and from amongst the most ferocious nations gathered congregations that were, if not in reality, yet in name and in some of their usages, Christians."

Efforts were made (we are told by the same historian) to rouse the Lutherans in imitation of the Roman Catholics to missionary enterprizes. But the situation of the Lutheran princes and various other causes, combined to make these efforts vain. "But the Reformed, (he remarks) and especially the English and Dutch, whose mercantile adventures carried them to the remotest parts of the world, and who planted extensive colonies during this century in Asia, Africa, and America, enjoyed the best advantages for extending the limits of the Christian Church. Nor did these nations wholly neglect this duty, although they are taxed with grasping at the wealth of the Indians, but neglecting their souls, and perhaps they did not perform so much as they might have done." Vol. iii, p. 294.

Here, then, for the first time, we come upon colonies in connection with the religious condition and prospects of heathen people; and certainly no great advantage appears to have arisen from them to the cause of the propagation of faith or opinions. We do not forget the missionary labours of that "Apostle to the Indians," John Eliot, nor of his noble compeers, the Mayhews; but we deny that their influence was that of colonists as distinguished from missionaries. We deny that their success in converting the Indians is any more to be attributed to the colonies of English around them, than the withering, blighting influence of those colonies of white men upon the Indians, is to be attributed to these missionaries. With as much justice the influence of the Christian missionaries in the Sandwich Islands may be attributed to the European and American settlers there, who are to a great extent, enemies of the missionaries and of Christianity!

It would, therefore, be altogether a new feature in the conduct of Christian missions to send out colonies with a view to converting heathen people. And not only would this be a new feature in the conduct of Christian Missions, but its being applied to Africa is a *singular* feature in this new missionary theory of the colonizationists. Only in reference to that continent, do they advocate colonization as an improvement upon preaching and teaching the gospel of Christ. We may depend on missionaries to do the work in all other countries, but in Africa it has to be done by colonies!

This new theory of Foreign Missions, is contrary to all modern as well as ancient missionary experience. We assert, and we do it with full knowledge of what we say, that missionaries in heathen countries now, do not find the presence of Englishmen, or of Americans generally, any advantage to them in their work. Indeed, they consider it a hindrance, except in those few cases in which these parties are men of decided and consistent piety. And the reason is obvious. The inconsistent conduct, the dishonesty, or the sabbath-breaking of one such American, whether seaman or merchant, or consul, speaks to the natives more powerfully against Christianity than many sermons of the missionary can speak in its favour. Missionaries would generally, much prefer to be alone among the heathen than to have irreligious compatriots near them. The want of their protection and their society, they consider a small evil, compared with the hindrance of their presence and example. And how much more certainly, must the influence and example of irreligious colonists always counterwork and oppose all the good instructions of good men in the colony.

There can be no doubt whatever, to any one who has had any experience in such affairs, or who will carefully consider the subject, that a colony of settlers from another country speaking another language, and belonging to another nation, and professing another religion, (even though their complexion may be the same with that of the natives) must, in a thousand ways, come into collision and conflict with them; and that the consequence must be mutual jealousy and hatred and strife, so, that in the end, one or the other must succumb. All these difficulties attend the effort to propagate Christianity by colonists in distinction from missionaries. The colonist is very apt to be their enemy, but the missionary is the friend of the heathen. He lives for them. He dies for them. He has renounced home and friends for them. He is devoted to their good and is their servant for Christ's sake. And they know that these things are so.

In confirmation of these remarks upon the inevitable mutual jealousy and hatred of natives and colonists, we quote Mr. Wilson's kind and cautious hints to the Colonization Society:

"There are some things connected with the management of these settlements, as well as the manner in which trade is conducted, that are very prejudicial to the improvement of the natives, and they ought to be corrected." Page 442.

"Another object which ought to be kept constantly before the minds of those who feel an interest in the general welfare of the country is, that the moral and religious improvement of the natives should be cared for as well as that of the Liberians. If one class is educated and improved to the neglect of the other, then the neglected one must be doomed to the task of drawing water and hewing wood all the days of their life ; and their fate must be that of all other barbarous tribes who have been brought in contact with civilized men without the intervention of the gospel." Page 410.

"In consequence, however, of frequent collisions between the colonists and the natives, which kept the minds of the latter in an unfit state to receive religious impressions; and in consequence of the jealousy with which the colonists looked upon the efforts of the missionaries to raise the natives in the scale of civilization and intelligence; and in consequence of legislation which had the tendency to embarrass the labours of the missionaries, the mission was transferred to the Gabun in 1842, where it has been carried on efficiently ever since." Page 501.

We quote also, to the same effect, some remarks from the pen, we suppose, of a coloured man in Liberia, copied from the Liberia Herald of June 18, 1856:

"I am very sorry for this spirit, too prevalent among Americo-Liberians, who are, by the way, overrun with missionaries, while thousands and tens of thousands of natives are perishing for lack of knowledge. It is time, high time, for Churches and Boards to say, 'So I turn to the Gentiles.' In my humble opinion, gospel fat, gospel foundered, gospel sick, gospel free, and gospel hardened; the gospel thrown away in the street until loathed as it were; how can any other feeling toward missionaries prevail among those who look only at the bread they eat, and envy what they do not give!"

"Should God turn these blessings into a curse, while three and four missionaries are stationed among some two or three hundred Americo-Liberians, and three and four denominations at work in one small hamlet, we should not repine. The missionaries are not to be blamed; they are sent. In the mean time, whole tribes of ten and twenty thousand native Liberians, (all destined, I hope, to be one nation and one people,) hear not the preacher's cry, 'Come over and help us.' No *book-man* sits before their children, and when schools are sent them, the same ignorant gabbers say, 'better send them powder, and shot, and fire, and death;' 'wasting money,' 'eating up means,' 'making them more able to cheat and rob,' 'bigger rascals, and villains.' And just as it goes; what teachers ever taught boys wickedness? Alas! for men, I believe the duties of the church to be marked out by God. I do not expect to see the good only of civilization and education. There is evil in Christian nations, evil and good seem to go together, tares and the wheat are in the same field, and the bad apparently looks the prevailing thing; evil ever had the majority, and when will the world be better?"

"A Traveller."

This "Traveller," of whatever complexion he may be, is evidently a man of sense. There is great good sense in his last remark that, there is always evil in Christian nations mixed with the good and predominating over it, and that we must not expect to see only what is good in civilization or education. If we send only civilization (and that but half civilized itself,) to Africa we m st not expect that we shall see "only good," or even chiefly good, come out of it. The heathen of Africa to be made better, need a mightier influence than civilization; the influence of Divine illumination and grace.

Some of the orators of the Society represent every colonist at Liberia as a missionary! So far is this from being true, if the judgment and experience of wise and good men may be taken, (men who have for years, directed the affairs of Foreign Missions from these United States to all the heathen world) that we have heard them say they never knew a single coloured man in this country, whom they would be willing to commission as a missionary to the heathen! Coloured men to be preachers to the colonists they had sent out; but to go alone amongst the heathen, as missionaries, they had never known any that were fit. And yet persons who have had no experience in the conduct of Foreign Missions imagine that every colonist that is sent forth to Liberia is a missionary of Christianity! These simple hearted persons know very little of the nature and circumstances of heathen society, or they would be less sanguine of the results of indiscriminately thrusting forth poor, unprepared, free negroes upon it. There is not a Missionary Society in this country, that has had even twenty years experience, but has been led to feel more and more impressed with the necessity of more carefully selecting even the ministers of the gospel whom it sends forth. And the reason is, because *some ministers*, even educated men and men approved at home, have been found unable to pass unhurt through the ordeal that awaited them amongst the heathen. Yet here is a Society that will receive from any planter in South Carolina, one hundred negroes for their colonies to-morrow, if he will pay (or if the Society can beg the money to pay) their passage and six months provisions; and these one hundred negroes, good, bad, and indifferent, are to be considered so many missionaries of the gospel of Christ! Well may Mr. Wilson say:

"The idea of gathering up coloured people indiscriminately, in this country, and setting them down upon the shores of Africa, with the design or expectation that they will take the lead in diffusing a pure Christianity among the natives, deserves to be utterly rejected by every friend of Africa. A proposition to transport white men in the same indiscriminate manner to some other heathen country, with the view of evangelizing the natives of that country, would be regarded, to say the least, as highly extravagant." Page 507.

Upon what principle of sober sense can such rash proceedings be approved? Who can doubt that every company of blacks sent out thus, from a Southern plantation, or from a Northern city or community, carries out at least, twenty fold more of the world, and the flesh, and the devil, than of Christian character, or of the experience of God's grace in the heart? And are the world, and the flesh, and the devil, in the hearts of poor, ignorant, depraved men, so very different in Africa, from what they are in America, that the sending forth of a cargo of such influences is to be considered a Christian missionary operation?

The Lord Jesus Christ himself, was the author of Christian missions. He ordained a very simple means for the conversion of the world. It was just preaching and teaching. "Go teach all nations," said he. And the Apostle Paul, himself a most distinguished and successful missionary, tells us that the means appointed by the Lord Jesus Christ to this end, is just "the *foolishness of preaching.*" "We preach, (said he,) Christ crucified, to the Jews a stumbling block and to the Greeks foolishness, but to them who are called both Jews and Greeks, Christ the power of God and the wisdom of God." This is a very simple means. But it is employed by an almighty agent, the Divine Spirit, who accompanies the faithful use of it, all the world over, with his omnipotent grace. It is this omnipotent influence of the Spirit of God, which alone can do anything for the heathen. And He will be honoured by us in the employment of what He devises and reveals, or else His blessing shall be withheld. If we substitute a new and a different means from that which the Head of the church has promised to bless, we must not expect his blessing. The Colonization Society may move heaven and earth, may enlist the general government, and all the people of this country, in the scheme of sending the free blacks to Africa, and they may urge on the movement by pleading that it alone can and will christianize Africa. But let it not be expected that all this effort and noise can change the ordinance of Jesus Christ. It pleases God, by the foolishness of preaching, to save them that believe, and by nothing else; especially by nothing that man devises, and in which the wisdom and the contrivance of man are seen conspicuous.

We do not undertake to say, that the missionaries by whom Africa is to be converted to God, must be white men, any more than we can allow others to say they must necessarily be black men. God will raise up whom he will for that work. But what we do say is, that according to the Bible and all church history, God will convert Africa in no other way than he has converted, or will convert any other country, viz: by the foolishness of preaching, and by the doctrine of the cross, and by the use of men called by him to preach this preaching, and to teach this doctrine.

In conclusion, we must be permitted to say to the Colonization Society, that they should learn a lesson from the "steamships effort," to beware of rash measures, and of rash men. The colony might well say of the Society, "Save me from my friends," and the Society might well say the same of the Naval Committee of the House of Representatives, that agreed to urge for them that gigantic measure. Legislative benevolence is always the most fumbling and bungling benevolence in the world. The greatest enemies of the Society and its colonies, need not have desired them any greater misfortune, than the adoption of that mad report would have been. The Society have put their hand to a work whose very magnitude and difficulties should make them sober. Let them beware of rash councils, and hasty plans. Let them eschew the great swelling words to which the writers of their reports, and the orators of their annual meetings have been so much addicted. We know not, nor do they, whether the Providence that brought the negroes here, intends to take them, even those now free, back to Africa or not. If He designs it to be done, His hand will do it, for no mortal's can. If He designs to bless the African race with Christianity, He will do that also, for it is beyond the power of man. And of one thing we may be sure, that the methods by which He will accomplish this latter object, never will be found to be the employment of darkness to enlighten darkness, or corruption to purify corruption. And though He may make use of some of Africa's own children, to raise their mother up from degradation, they will, doubtless, be men who have personally experienced another transformation, than any which a mere removal from America to Africa can work in the Colonists of Liberia.